OP

9/99

4ºº

I0958083

Other books by Sally Pierson Dillon:
  The Code Breaker
  Crossroads in Time (Andrews University Press)
  Little Hearts for Jesus
  Making the Bible a Delight (GC Ministerial Association)
  Michael Asks Why (Pacific Press)

To order, **call 1-800-765-6955.**
Visit us at *www.rhpa.org* for information on other Review and Herald products.

THE AMAZING
TRUE STORY OF
THE GREAT CONTROVERSY

SALLY PIERSON DILLON

REVIEW AND HERALD® PUBLISHING ASSOCIATION
HAGERSTOWN, MD 21740

Copyright © 2000 by
Review and Herald® Publishing Association
International copyright secured
All rights reserved

The author assumes full responsibility for the accuracy of all facts
and quotations as cited in this book.

This book was
Edited by Andy Nash
Copyedited by Eugene Lincoln
Designed by Willie S. Duke
Electronic makeup by Shirley M. Bolivar
Cover art by Greg and Tim Hildebrandt
Typeset: 12.5/16 Berkley Book

PRINTED IN U.S.A.
04 03 02 01 00   5 4 3 2 1

R&H Cataloging Service
Dillon, Sally Pierson, 1959-
    War of the invisibles: the amazing true story of the great controversy.

    1. Church history—Juvenile works.   2. Second Coming—Juvenile works.
3. Eschatology—Juvenile works.   I. Title.

                        270

ISBN 0-8280-1549-X

DEDICATION

To my friends Mary Ramos and Virginia Smith, and my husband, Bruce, who insisted, "You should write a book to get kids excited about the 'Great Controversy'!"

To my online friend, Juanita Sossong-Lesko, who affectionately named her guardian angel Mark. Even though the cancer infiltrated her brain and she was sometimes confused, her last words were addressed to Mark as she lapsed in and out of consciousness: "Is it time to wake up yet? Is Jesus coming for us?"

To Marian Forschler and Denise Small-Conche, the other two charter members of my online Sabbath school class, who gave me encouragement and support during this project.

And to my boys, Don and Mike, who prepared me for this when they were little boys by repeatedly begging for "back-in-time" stories.

Contents

MARK

IMMORTAL WATCHER

. . . God is love; God is love.
Praise Him, praise Him,
All ye little children . . .

 just can't get that song out of my head. Ever since I first heard it, I've just loved it, even if it is only simple human music. Of course, around here we sing it, "Praise Him! Praise Him! All ye mighty angels. . . ."

Hello. My name is Mark. Actually, that is not my real name, but in the limited dimension of human speech, that is the closest I could come up with.

I am a watcher. I work for the Most High and observe the choices of men and women on Planet Earth. There are many of us, each assigned to cover different areas—and people. We document the progress of the war and the choices of the humans involved. We are usually invisible to the human eye, unless the Most High gives specific instructions to decloak our spirit images so that we can appear to the spiritually sensitive humans. Usually these are humans on the side of the Most High, though occasionally we appear to the humans on the enemy side. In such cases, we appear as warriors and frighten them into retreat, thus preventing injury to the humans siding with the Most High.

Unfortunately, we often scare the people we are protecting too, and we have to say continually, "Don't be afraid." If you don't believe me, check out the biblical human records. Every time we appear, it's "Don't be afraid" or "Fear not." As an observer, I am rarely called to appear to humans. The guardians usually get that job.

You would call me an immortal. It's a silly term—all of us were created to be immortal. The only reason humans are not immortal is because of their continued poor choices. I have covered human choices and transmitted them to the heavenly archives since the dawn of the earthly phenomenon called time.

The Most High has instructed me to make these records available to you and His other humans before "human time" is finished. They will aid you in your struggles in the final conflict on earth and will be a source of great encouragement. It is as if the book had already been written, and you can peek ahead and see exactly what will happen next. You can see that the Most High will be victorious in the end, no matter how frustrating your present circumstances.

Obviously, my records have been greatly abbreviated to enable you to actually read through them, and simplified to make the outcomes understandable to the human mind.

As you read these, take courage, human one. The Most High and all of His hosts of warriors, protectors, observers, and other created beings watch your struggles and choices with keen interest. Do not be discouraged. Peek at the end of the book and know that the Most High will be honored in the end, both by those who worship Him and by those who don't. We cheer and applaud your efforts. Remember, no matter how grim your circumstances seem, you are not alone.

JOE

ROME, A.D. 67

he stabbing pain in his side grew stronger, and his lungs screamed for air as Joe sprinted around the corner. The mob was close on his heels. Frantically he dodged into a doorway and disappeared. The mob surged around the corner and passed the doorway into the street. "Where did he go? Where did he go?" they cried.

Joe held his breath as the mob passed, then he carefully moved a trunk from the corner of the room. It was an ordinary trunk—like any other trunk in that part of town where the family kept their few belongings. Under the trunk was a trap door. He quickly opened it and dropped through, pulling it shut behind him. There was no one to replace the trunk over the trap door, and he hoped Cornelius would come home first and not be angry with him for leaving it that way. It was an emergency; it couldn't be helped. He dropped into the tunnel and started walking westward. Several minutes passed before his eyes got used to the darkness.

As adaptable as his eyes were, being human he couldn't see the guardians who stood at the door while he moved the trunk and opened the trap door. Nor could he see them maintaining their vigil over the tiny apartment that concealed the entrance to the underground maze of tunnels known as the catacombs.

Ignoring the pain in his side, Joe continued to move briskly down the tunnels. Carefully he counted his paces so that he would know where to turn in the darkness. As he rounded another corner he saw a glow up ahead. He pressed eagerly toward it. In a hollowed-out room sat several believers.

"Joseph," gasped Anna, running over to him. "You are safe! We've been quite worried about you." The guardian standing by Anna smiled, and I nodded.

Of course you've been worried, I thought. *That's why the guardians impressed you to pray for Joe—to give them permission to protect him.*

"God is good," Joe said breathlessly. "He spared my life and helped me escape, but they got Marcus."

Anna let out a little cry. "Marcus?" The other believers surged forward to comfort Anna. "Oh, my brother, my brother," she sobbed.

"You must be strong," Joe said. "Marcus would want you to. Marcus loves the Lord, and if it means giving his life, he will."

"I know," Anna sobbed. "I know he loves the Lord, and I know the Lord loves him. It's just that it seems so unfair. We've been accused of these horrible things that none of us have done, and then we get sentenced to death. And it's not as if . . . as if it's an execution, where we're allowed to mourn for them. We're executed for entertainment at parties and for fun. It's bad enough to imagine my brother suffering without imagining the crowds cheering and clapping as he cries in agony."

"Stop!" Joe exclaimed. "Those kinds of thoughts aren't going to help you. We need to keep our minds fixed on Jesus and His promises, or it will make us crazy." The other believers nodded.

I smiled at the guardians as we watched the little band of believers press together and pray even more earnestly. The enemy had been particularly cruel and had been creative in finding ways of killing and torturing the believers, and yet instead of driving them away from God, persecution just drew them closer to Him and to each other. One more failure for the rebellion. God's people remained loyal. While it is hard being a recorder of such suffering, it is encouraging to see the steadfast loyalty from humans who had been apparently weak until this point. Joe was right. God is good!

MARCUS: MAMERTINE PRISON, ROME, A.D. 67

Marcus leaned against the stone-cold wall in the damp Roman prison cell. He touched the bruises on his arm gingerly. "I guess I'll live," he muttered to himself. His eyes were adjusting to the darkness, and as he glanced around he realized he was not alone.

The others in the cell seemed divided into two groups. There was a small loose knot of men on one side and three or four tough-looking loners standing around by themselves. Marcus sat in silence. He was not sure that being in a jail cell would be any safer than being in the hands of those who had beaten him and brought him here. Was he in a room with murderers and criminals, or were these other believers, who were in here for the same reason he was?

After a short time, one left the small group in the corner and approached Marcus timidly. "What brings you here, young man?" he asked. Marcus looked up at him, trying to form an answer.

The huge man leaning against the wall on the other side laughed harshly. "Same thing as the rest of us, you idiot!" he said. "This part of the jail is only for the most toughened criminals. We are being saved for something special." He glanced at Marcus. "This one does look pretty young and scrawny to be a bandit, though. Perhaps he's just a pickpocket who annoyed someone particularly important."

Marcus shook his head. "I'm no thief."

"Oh," the big man said respectfully. "A wily murderer. You're more dangerous than you look."

The older man, who had approached Marcus first, backed timidly toward his corner. Marcus stood painfully, holding onto the wall for support. The room seemed to spin around him, but soon his vision cleared. "No," he replied, "I am in here for being a follower of The Way."

The big man spat on the floor. "A Christian?"

The older man now rushed toward Marcus. "You are among friends," he said. "There are five of us here."

"Christians?" Marcus asked.

"Why, yes. Perhaps we know some of the same people." He put his arm around Marcus' shoulders and shepherded him toward their corner. The other loners looked at each other and shook their heads.

"Well," one said, "this used to be a prison for the toughest criminals. Now we have to share it here with all these religious weaklings who are too insane to realize what their choices will cost them."

The old man drew himself to his full height and turned to face them. "No," he replied. "We are not too insane to know what our choices cost, but we give our lives gladly for One who gave His life for us. We know what we're doing."

The second loner looked at the first and shook his head. "I know why *we're* in here," he muttered. "But these weaklings frighten me." The other tough nodded, and although the cell was small, the distance between the two groups seemed to widen.

The guardians smiled. Even these degenerate toughs in a prison cell could sense the power of the Mighty One through these Christians. The guardians would not have to do any physical protecting today. Just the sense of His power was enough.

* * *

"On your feet, Christians!" the soldier shouted. "It's time to go."

Marcus struggled to his feet. The older man who had befriended him squeezed his arm and whispered, "Blessed are you when you are persecuted for my sake. Rejoice and be exceedingly glad, for great is your reward in heaven."

Marcus smiled. "We've got heavy rewards coming, friend."

The soldier shook his head. These Christians were spooky to deal with. Some of them insisted on being crucified upside down because they "weren't good enough" to die the way their Christ had been crucified. Some wouldn't die no matter what they had done to them, and they were sent to work in the quarries on the island of Patmos. All of them acted as if other beings were around. It was just creepy. The soldier would rather fight a hundred barbarians than deal with these strange folk.

Marcus and his friends broke into song as the soldiers marched them from the prison to the palace. The closer they got to the palace, the louder their singing became.

"Didn't your God tell you that you were supposed to be the light of the world?" one soldier sneered. "This is the closest you'll come to that! You're going to be the light of Nero's banquet!"

Marcus tried not to listen and just sang louder. "If that's the kind of light You want me to be, God," he prayed silently, "then that's all right with me. Just help me to be brave and not embarrass You. I want to be a good representative for You."

The soldiers dragged the little group to the stakes strategically placed around the banqueting area. Wood was already piled around them. They chained one man to each stake and then doused all of them with heavy black oil. As the soldier leaned forward to light Marcus's wood with his torch, Marcus began to shake. His guardian drew closer and placed his hands around the boy's shoulders.

"Look up! Look up!" he whispered.

Marcus turned his face skyward. "I see Him! I see Him!" he cried. The other human torches were looking up too, their faces strangely lighted.

A booming voice surrounded them: "Be thou faithful unto death, and I will give thee a crown of life." They were filled with joy and comfort and, as the breath left their bodies, the guardians and I both heaved a sigh of relief. In their human consciousness, in their next split second, they would see the Holy One coming in the clouds, and they would be rising to meet Him in the air—rising with new bodies: no more pain, no more suffering.

I smiled as I turned from the grim scene. How good our Master is! How faithful never to let the weakest of His followers die alone without encouragement!

EPILOGUE

Though Marcus and many others died for their faith, Joe, Anna, and others carried on, and the little groups in the catacombs grew faster than Nero's persecution could kill them off. The guardians were not always allowed to save the lives of those they cared for, but they were always with them. And the Almighty never left them alone during their difficult times.

Miriam

Miriam's hands pushed the grinding stone rhythmically as she tried not to think about what her mother was saying.

"We can't get onions or lentils or melons in the market. We are almost out of dried fruit. Soon all we will be having is bread and water for our meals."

Grandpa chuckled.

"What are you laughing about, old man?" Mama demanded.

"He promised only that our bread and water would be sure," replied Grandpa with a twinkle. "I don't remember anything about melons or onions."

"Very funny," Mama snapped. She added some wood to the fire in the little domed oven. "Eventually this siege is going to starve us into submission."

Miriam looked at Grandpa. He smiled at her reassuringly. "It is almost time to go," he said. "We must be ready."

"That is a bad idea," replied Mama. "The Goldman family tried to escape last week, and the Romans did terrible things to them. Anna says Simon saw it from the wall, and it was just horrible. They are some of the cruelest people in the world!"

"Jesus said that we would have a sign," Grandpa answered gently. "When Jerusalem is surrounded by armies, it will be time. I'm sure His Holy Spirit will let us know when we should run, and when it is time, we must not dally."

Miriam's grandfather was a follower of Jesus, human Son of the Most High. He had been a child when Jesus was living among humans and had even loved Him. He had raised Miriam's father to be a believer too.

As with most families, some members had more trust in the Most High than others. Miriam's mother had a strong sense of responsibility and worried continually about running the household since her mother-in-law had died and she had taken over. The siege had continued for weeks, and she was nearing panic over their dwindling food supplies.

The door to the courtyard opened, and Miriam's father and brother entered. "What did they say at the Temple?" Grandpa asked. Miriam stopped grinding to listen.

"The prophet stood at the top of the steps and told us that Jerusalem is the Lord's footstool. His Temple is holy, and He will never allow it to be destroyed," Papa answered.

"Yes, and all the people cheered and shouted," Seth added. "The priests blew a horn, and everyone rejoiced."

"What about all the soldiers surrounding our city?" Mama asked.

"The prophet says the Lord will do something about them—we just don't know what. Remember all the stories? Remember Elijah and Elisha and the other prophets? God was always getting rid of enemy armies. He has lots of experience with that." Papa's eyes twinkled just as Grandpa's did when he was excited.

"But . . ." Miriam interrupted.

"Yes?" Papa answered.

"I thought Jesus told us that Jerusalem *would* be destroyed. Remember the time Grandpa told us about His riding in through the Sheep Gate on the donkey and crying, for Jerusalem would be all torn up because they would not listen to Him?"

Grandpa nodded. "You're right. I believe this must be a false prophet. His prophecy doesn't match what Jesus told us."

"But he quoted the Scriptures," Seth protested. "The Psalms and the old prophets. He sounded like a true prophet to me."

Grandpa shook his head. Papa's lips pulled into a thin, straight line. Then he shook his shoulders as if to change the subject. "What did you find out at the market?" he asked Grandpa.

"It's pretty dismal. There are many families with gold to trade—just no merchants with food to trade the gold for."

"Our supplies are getting low," Mama added. "I did buy these, though." She pulled out four daggers from her basket.

Everyone looked surprised. "I didn't see you buy those," Grandpa exclaimed.

"I know. You were talking with the other men. I feel that we need protection. This loving-our-neighbors stuff is good during peacetime, but as people get more hungry, human life has less value. I am afraid that if they run out of food before we do, they will try to steal ours." She gave a dagger to each male and tucked the last one into her sash.

"This is really neat!" Seth exclaimed. "A real dagger of my very own!"

Papa turned his over and over in his hands. "I do not think we should rely on this kind of protection," he said slowly. "What do you think, Father?"

"We never have had weapons in our home," Grandpa answered. "I do not want to start now. The Lord has always taken care of us and provided for us. I believe He will continue to do so. To arm ourselves like this is to insult Him and to show that we don't believe He really can take care of us."

"You men are so impractical!" Mama sputtered. "Just what are you going to do when some starving neighbors come beating the door down demanding food?"

"Feed them what we still have," Grandpa answered firmly.

Papa looked hard at the dagger. "This piece is well made," he commented. "Perhaps we can trade it in the market for something else of value." Then to Mama he continued, "You have always had an eye for fine workmanship."

Mama was not to be complimented. She snorted and turned her back to the men. Seth turned the dagger over and over, running his hands over the tooled silver and gently running his thumb along the razor-sharp blade. Seth's shoulders drooped as he saw Papa hand his dagger to Grandpa. Slowly he gave his to Grandpa too.

Seth was young and confused by the prophet at the Temple, but he loved God and was obedient to the wishes of his father even though he would rather have kept the dagger. The Most High never leaves those with a tender, sincere heart to the enemy. I knew Seth would be given every chance to escape—and the time was near.

The city was thick with guardians as well as deceiving spirits. This was the planet's core of action at this point in human time. We all waited tensely.

* * *

"Grandpa," Miriam asked, "exactly what did Jesus say about this time? What are we supposed to be watching for, and what are we supposed to do?"

Grandpa smiled. "Come, let's sit in the shade where we can talk."

When they were comfortable, Grandpa began. "Jesus was

telling His disciples about these times. He said, 'A time is coming when you will see armies surround Jerusalem.'"

"That's now!" Miriam exclaimed.

"Yes," Grandpa replied. "Jesus told us, 'Then you will know that it will soon be destroyed. Those in Judea should then escape to the mountains. Those in the city should get out. Those in the country should not enter the city. This is a time when God will punish Jerusalem. Everything will come true, just as it has been written.'"*

"If we left right now, wouldn't the Romans kill us as they did those other people?" Miriam asked anxiously.

"Maybe," Grandpa replied. "I think we need to be ready to go soon, though. When the time comes, we won't have time for anything. Jesus told us, 'No one on the roof should go down into his house to take anything out. No one in the field should go back to get his coat.'"

"Does that mean that we need to just leave without packing anything?" Miriam asked.

"I think so," Grandpa said. "If our God can get us safely out of a besieged city, then He can surely take care of us once we escape without our earthly goods."

"Do Mama and Papa know this?" Miriam asked earnestly.

"Of course," Grandpa answered. "I love your Mama and Papa, and I would not keep such an important secret from them. I worry, though. A lot of different ideas are being tossed around in the city, and your father has been discussing them. Sometimes I am afraid he feels torn between what our religious leaders tell him and what Jesus told us."

"But Jesus is God's Son! Surely His warnings count the most!"

"Yes, they do. But we Jews have such a long tradition, and in any religion it is very hard to go against what the leaders and traditions say, even if you know for sure that what you are learning is true."

I smiled. Miriam's grandfather was right. Humans have struggled with that issue throughout time. Perhaps it is because their religious leaders, no matter how well-intentioned, are still human. They make mistakes. It seems that the more authority they have, the more vulnerable they become to pride and arrogance. This leads them to be more interested in developing their own power instead of worshiping the Almighty One.

"We will pray about it and then leave everything up to God," Grandfather said. "He does not want you to spend all your time worrying and being afraid. We know that for sure!"

Miriam laughed. "Yes, I'll just be a lily of the field."

"You are every bit as pretty as His field lilies," agreed Grandpa. "You are His city lily."

* * *

"Wake up! Wake up!" Mama's voice seemed like it was coming from far away as Miriam struggled to consciousness. Mama was dressed and in the courtyard shouting to the rest of the family. "The city gates are open!"

Papa's voice replied, "How can that be? We are under siege. The gate weighs so much it takes 20 men to open it. It is secured by huge iron bars in solid stone!"

"Weird things are happening!" Mama said. "There is a strange light over the altar at the Temple, and some people say they have seen golden chariots in the clouds. Anna says the Romans have left. Come right now! They have left their camps outside the city wall, with all their supplies and everything."

Grandpa entered the family sleeping chamber and helped Miriam to her feet. Papa and Seth were already throwing on their outer cloaks. It was after midnight, and the air was chilly.

"Is it time?" Miriam asked.

Grandpa nodded. They all rushed to the courtyard.

"We need to grab some baskets so we have something to bring back the spoils in," Mama instructed them.

"No," Papa replied. "We need to take a lamb to the Temple right away as a thank offering to God for chasing away our enemies."

"No," Grandpa said firmly. "It is the time Jesus told us about. We don't have time for anything. We need to leave the city now."

"And go where?" Mama asked.

"East. We will cross the Jordan and hide in the mountains on the other side."

"No way! There are bandits over there. There is food aplenty now outside the walls free for the taking, and we are wasting time standing here talking about it."

Papa took a deep breath. "I have been praying for this day. I am going to the Temple to offer a sacrifice. You all do what you feel is right, but this I must do. Seth, come with me."

Seth looked at the ground. "I believe Grandpa," he said slowly. "If Jesus said we didn't have time even to go inside and pack, then I don't think we have time for sacrifices. Grandpa always told us that Jesus was the last sacrifice and that we only need to pray to God now. I want to go with Grandpa. Please come with us, Papa!"

Mama snorted. "I am getting food for the rest of you religious fanatics! I never minded your Christian ways before because they were a lot easier than our cumbersome Jewish laws, but this is no time for religion. Come, Miriam!"

Miriam placed her hand in Grandpa's large one. "I want to go with Grandpa and Seth. Jesus warned us about this, and this is the time. We need to go. Please come with us, Mama."

Mama turned, walked out of the courtyard door into the street, and slammed it. Grandpa looked at Papa. "Please, son. Don't forget everything you learned at my knee." Grandpa's eyes filled with tears, but he stood tall and rigid.

Papa stood silent. "Oh, please, God," Miriam whispered. "Please save my papa!"

Suddenly Papa reached for Miriam's other hand. "Well, what are we waiting for?" he said. "There's no time to waste! Let's head for the Jordan!" The four of them beamed at each other, then rushed for the courtyard door and spilled into the crowded streets.

EPILOGUE

I happily followed the little band as they fled the city. Most of the inhabitants were celebrating: some in the Temple, some on the fields raiding the Romans' leftovers, some dancing in the streets. All of the sincere followers of the Son knew this was the moment, though, and all of them were guided safely across the Jordan and into the mountains. Not one was lost or left behind. There they formed a Christian community that grew and eventually sent missionaries throughout the empire sharing the good news about the Son of the Most High and His love for humans.

My recording task was much more pleasant than other recorders at that time. My friend recording in the city told of terrible suffering. Miriam's mother had indeed found supplies and had restocked her stores. But as surprising as their departure was, the reappearance of the Roman army was even more so. The siege resumed as the Jews were celebrating the Passover in Jerusalem. All the celebrating stopped.

The siege continued where it had left off earlier—except without God's people. Terrible stories of families turning on each other, neighbors killing others for food, starvation, torture, and death leaked from the city.

Then Jerusalem fell. The beautiful Temple—the pride of the Jewish nation—went up in flames as those inside burned, ankle deep in the blood of their compatriots. No wonder the Son had cried when He foresaw this. He had warned them. He had begged them to follow Him, to come out, to be safe. But they would not.

Through the worst times, the Most High always cares for His own. They are His chosen ones. The problem has never been His remembering His people, but whether or not they choose to be His.

---

* See Luke 21:20-22.

Peter

eter! Peter!" a little girl's voice called out. "Papa says to bring the sheep in a little bit early this afternoon."

"Papa's back?" Peter asked.

"Yes," she replied. "He got in a little while ago. He and Mama say they want to talk to you about something important."

Peter whistled to his dog, and they started to round up the stragglers and herd the group back toward home. This took some doing. Living in a particularly rugged vale in the Alps was not easy. It was rocky, and sometimes Peter had to take the sheep a long way to find grass. The way back was steep and slippery, and the sheep were clumsy and not very smart.

"What do you think it is?" his little sister asked excitedly.

Peter shrugged. "Maybe he's going to let me sell some things in the village and let you watch the sheep."

"But it's not time for shearing the sheep," his little sister protested, "and we usually don't take cheeses into the village until we have a full cartload."

Peter nodded. "That's true. Perhaps Papa found a place to buy more soaps and jewels. Perhaps he's going to let me go on the road with him as a peddler."

His little sister frowned. "You know Mama wouldn't agree to that. She thinks you're too young even to sell wool and cheese in the market."

"Well, I'm not!" announced Peter defensively. "I'm a man now. I'm already 13."

His sister laughed. "You may be a man, but you aren't as big as Papa yet."

"Well, I will be soon," Peter growled.

It seemed like hours before he and his little sister herded all the sheep into the enclosure and were able to drag the gate across the opening.

"OK, now we will find out," Peter said. They hurried toward the house—a small room built onto the front of a cave that split deep into the rock. It was much larger inside than it appeared from the front.

Every time Peter's family prepared for a selling trip, they would work late into the night copying portions of Scripture to share with their customers. Then Mama would fold these up and sew them inside the hemlines of their cloaks. For a long time now Scripture had been outlawed in Christian countries.

"Papa, why does the church not allow us to have access to all of the Scriptures?" Peter asked. "It seems that it would be much easier to follow what God wanted if all people could read it themselves and know what He said."

Papa shook his head. "Perhaps it's because that is not as important to the Christian church today as their own power is."

"What do you mean?" Peter asked.

"Well," Papa explained, "the church leaders have said that common people should not be allowed to read the Scriptures because they might interpret them incorrectly. This means that only church leaders can tell us what God really wants us to do."

"But how do we know *they* are right?" Peter asked.

"We don't," Papa answered grimly. "As we have copied portions of Scripture here illegally, we've found many places where we believe they are wrong."

"Like what?" Peter asked curiously.

"One thing," Papa began, "is the Sabbath." Peter nodded. He knew that his family worshiped God on a different day than the people down in the valleys and in the cities. Christians in the cities worshiped on Sunday.

"Why did they change?" Peter asked. "Or has it always been this way?"

"Oh, no," Papa said. "Jesus was a Jew. It was His habit to go to the synagogue every Sabbath. And for a few hundred years after Jesus went back to heaven, most Christians still worshiped on Sabbath. However, the pagans around them were sun worshipers. Their day for worshiping the sun was one big party. Sabbathkeeping was a much more serious affair. The pagans looked as if they were having a lot more fun. They started referring to the Sabbath as 'that old Jewish Sabbath.' The leaders of the Christian church decided to switch and to celebrate on Sunday, saying that they were celebrating Jesus' resurrection, even though there is no place in the Scriptures that Jesus ever asked them to change."

"But," Peter's little sister piped up, "not everyone knows that is not in the Bible. If the priests tell people that's what God wants them to do, then the people will believe it."

"This is true," Papa replied. "Many people really love God and are trying to please Him by worshiping on Sunday because they don't know that is not what He asks."

"What other things have you found in the Scriptures?" Peter asked.

"Well," Papa continued, "when Jesus went back to heaven, the Bible says He went back to be our High Priest."

"I know about high priests," Peter announced. "You've told us about them in our Bible stories. And you've told me all about Aaron, the first high priest, and lots of other ones."

"Do you know what a priest does?" Mama asked.

"He kills lambs," Peter's little sister volunteered.

"Yes," Mama replied. "He did that in the Old Testament. But more than that, he was a mediator."

"What is that?" Peter asked.

"A mediator is a person who talks to both sides when there is a conflict. He tries to bring both sides together," Mama explained. "A mediator must understand the thoughts and feelings of those on both sides of the conflict. Jesus is our Mediator. He is trying to help us become close friends with God again."

I smiled. If only all humans could understand how badly the Father wants to restore that friendship with them! If only they understood how much He was willing to give, how much He had given! The leaders of the church had done much to make people afraid of God—to make Him seem stern and angry and unforgiving. Even worse, most Christians believed them.

Peter's mother continued. "The leader of the official Christian church decided no one could approach God except through him. By doing that he is taking Jesus' job."

"Oh," Peter said. "I know that piece of Scripture: 'No one comes to the Father but by me.'"

"That's right," Mama answered. "But in the Christian churches today, people have to approach God through their church leaders and even then, those leaders want to approach God through Jesus' mother, Mary."

"Doesn't that hurt Jesus' feelings?" Peter's little sister asked.

"I'm sure it does," Mama answered.

Papa spoke. "Not only that, but the Christian leaders have added more requirements. They make people earn their forgiveness. Sometimes they have to go without food or be whipped or say special prayers over and over again. Others have to pay lots of money to church leaders in order to feel forgiven for their sins."

"But," Peter protested, his forehead wrinkling in thought, "I thought Jesus died for our sins, and that was all we need."

"That is true," Mama said. "But for hundreds of years people have been taught this instead. Most of these people love God and are working very hard to please Him, but they are worshiping idols, burning candles, saying the same prayers over and over again, and paying lots of money to corrupt men—all to beg God not to be angry with them."

"That is sad," Peter commented.

"Yes," Mama said. "It has always been sad. But now you are old enough, my son, to help do something about it."

A funny feeling hit the pit of Peter's stomach. His eyes widened. His guardian drew close and placed his hand on Peter's shoulder. Peter was going to need extra courage, and his guardian was prepared to give it to him.

"What is it?" he asked. "What can I do?"

* * *

Peter's face paled, and the guardians drew even closer. "Me? Leave home? I don't want to go away," he said softly. "Why?"

Mama began to cry. "It's a long story," Papa said. "Your mama and I used to be a part of the main Christian church. My brother is a fairly important priest. He has sent for you. He works in a castle in the Alps, where some very important church people live. He is going to educate you and teach you how to be a clerk."

"I already know how to read and write," Peter said proudly.

"Yes," Papa agreed, "and you learn quickly, so you will do very well there."

"But why do I have to go?" asked Peter.

"Many years ago," Papa began, "there was a teacher named Berengarius. He taught many of the things Mama and I have taught you—things from the Scriptures where we believe some of the church leaders are wrong. We believed him. Your mama and I were excommunicated by our priest and had to hide here in the mountains. My brother found out our hiding place. He has agreed not to tell anyone, but he wants you to live with him so he can see that you get a proper church education. If we don't allow you to go, then he will turn us in, and the authorities may send soldiers to our valley, burn our homes, and take all the children here, as they have done in many other mountain valleys. If you go cooperatively, he promises they will leave our valley alone."

Mama flung her arms around Peter. "Peter, we have taught you everything you need to know. The Holy Spirit will be with you and will help you with everything. You will be a missionary just like Paul. And you know we love you and will be praying for you every single day. Perhaps you will actually teach some of them in that castle instead of their always teaching you."

"But be careful," Papa urged. "Always wait for the approval of the Holy Spirit before you speak. There is much danger in speaking the truth where you are going. He will give you wisdom, though, and protectors."

Peter squared his shoulders. "If it will help protect you and Papa, and if I am to be a missionary for the Lord, then I am happy to go," he said, trying furiously to swallow the huge lump in his throat.

"I am sewing you a new cloak," Mama said. "I will put plenty of Scripture verses in the seams and the hems so that you will have them when you need them."

I smiled. It does not take adults to be brave followers of the Most High. It just takes committed humans of any age. I knew I was going to have an exciting time recording Peter's adventures.

CASTLE CANOSSA, JANUARY, A.D. 1077

I watched Peter settle in quickly to his new home in the castle monastery. He missed his family terribly, but he was a fast learner and was fascinated with all of the things that happened in a modern castle. He was a very quiet lad and did not comment on the things that his papa had warned him about. So far his uncle had not questioned him about those details. He applied the same energy and serious thought to each task given to him as he had back at home copying Scriptures and tending sheep. Peter had already been given a clerk position, something unusual for one so young. This gave him even more opportunity to listen to the discussions of the important princes of the church who came through in their travels.

"Peter," his uncle called. "We need to tidy up the office and make everything in perfect readiness. His Holiness, Pope Gregory VII, is coming here for the winter!"

"The pope?" asked Peter in astonishment. "His Holiness, the head of the whole Christian church? His Holiness who just announced that he was perfect and had never and could never make a doctrinal mistake?"

"Yes," his uncle answered, frowning hard. "Why do you ask?"

Peter paused. He had read that Pope Gregory had made this statement and also had told people that the Scriptures said so. Peter had been a student of the Scriptures long before he had ever come to work at the monastery, and he knew that nothing in the Scriptures supported this claim. Only God is perfect.

Peter shook his head. "I was just wondering if that was whom we were talking about," he replied.

"Of course it is!" his uncle snapped. "He is our pope, and we need to have everything just right before he gets here."

His uncle put his arm around Peter and drew him to the side, whispering in a conspiratorial way. "His Holiness is very upset. You know that His Holiness and King Henry IV have been trading insults for quite some time. Henry had the nerve to call His Holiness 'Monk Hildebrand.' His Holiness declared Henry unfit to rule and had him excommunicated."

Peter drew in his breath sharply. *What a terrible thing!* he thought. *To be excommunicated means you can't talk to God anymore and that God will not have anything to do with you either.*

I drew in closer. Surely Peter knew the Most High better than that. Surely he knew that the Almighty One would not lose total interest in a human being just because another human being ruled it to be.

The guardians drew in closer too. "Your parents were excommunicated too," one whispered. "And you know they still communicate with the Most High." Peter's face relaxed. I was relieved. The lad had not forgotten the things he had learned at home.

"Well, anyway," his uncle continued in an excited whisper, "Henry thought he would be all right and would just ignore the excommunication, but the princes under him were so afraid of His Holiness that they have now refused to support him. Rumor has it that Henry is on his way here to the castle. His Holiness wants to get here first and get his court set up. I promise you there will be lots of action here!"

I nodded thoughtfully to myself. Of course there was action coming. That was why I was here to take the records. I noticed many more guardians throughout the castle. It was unfortunate that Peter's uncle and the others could not see them. Perhaps they would be more careful in their decision-making.

* * *

I watched Pope Gregory VII arrive at the castle with his huge retinue of priests, clerks, and servants. They were comfortably settled when word came that King Henry IV was on his way. The guards at the castle had already heard rumors and were ready for action. They lined the wall. The ammunition was ready. If Henry wanted to fight, they were prepared.

Henry didn't want to fight. With no support from the nobles in his country, he realized he had lost. Henry was there to apologize.

Peter stood on the wall, watching the flags and banners of Henry's retinue coming closer and closer. "Uncle," he asked. "Is it true that Henry is coming to apologize and make peace?"

"That is what our informants tell us," his uncle replied, "but we are prepared to fight just in case."

Peter nodded and then asked, "If he does apologize, won't His Holiness forgive him?"

His uncle laughed. "Not without rubbing his nose in it first," he said.

"What do you mean?" asked Peter, the same careful look crossing his face.

"Well," blustered his uncle, "you don't insult someone as important as His Holiness and think that you can just get away with it by asking forgiveness. Just who does Henry think he is?"

Peter didn't answer. He kept thinking about a piece of Scripture Mama had sewn into his cloak the night before he left home. "If we confess our sins, he is faithful and just to forgive us our sins and to cleanse us from all unrighteousness" (1 John 1:9). *If God was so willing to forgive us if we confessed, why would His representative here on earth not do the same?* Papa had taught Peter to be very careful about the questions he asked, so he said nothing and continued to watch.

Despite the soldiers' readiness for battle, there were no opportunities for them to sharpen their skills. The outer gates of the castle opened, and King Henry entered. The rest of his retinue was left to camp in the outer court, and only Henry was brought through the second gates to the inner court. The sky was darkening, and a cold wind whipped through the Alps, blowing snow off the roofs and sprinkling it liberally over those waiting in the courtyard. Peter was glad his uncle had given him a thick fur coat to put over his shoulders as they continued to watch.

Henry knelt in the snow and took off his shoes, his hat, and his outer cloak. Peter could not hear what he was saying, but it looked like he was being very humble. The soldiers removed the things he had taken off, and he remained on his knees.

"Aren't they going to let him come in?" Peter asked.

His uncle laughed. "No, I don't think so," he answered. "I think his holiness will wait until he is really sure King Henry is sorry."

"He is going to make the king stay in the snow barefoot with no hat or warm cloak?" Peter asked incredulously.

His uncle looked at him sharply. "Whose side are you on, anyway?" he demanded.

The guardians pulled in closer. Peter just looked down and wisely said nothing.

* * *

On the third day Peter's uncle called him. "I need you to take notes," he said. "Come to the great hall."

Peter gathered up his things and hurried behind his uncle. His uncle placed him at a side table where he could hear clearly.

I smiled. Now Peter and I shared the same kind of duties—recording the choices of others. King Henry IV was brought in. He was shivering, his feet blue, his lips cracked and bleeding, his hair encrusted in ice. He no longer looked like a majestic king but a pitiful shivering broken man. He knelt before Pope Gregory and begged for forgiveness. And after three days of demonstrating his power and authority, Pope Gregory granted it.

Peter frowned as he recorded the discussion for his uncle.

35

How could God's representative be so arrogant and proud and unforgiving? It seemed so unlike the God Papa had taught him about far away in their mountain cave house. Could it be that his holiness was just another political figure wanting to control others? Could it be that he was not really God's chosen leader for this time? Peter knew those were questions he could never ask out loud.

But I knew. And if Peter waited patiently, the Most High would answer all of his questions. Before long King Henry, having regained the support of all his nobility, became powerful again. He returned and ousted Pope Gregory from his job, and he installed his own pope in Gregory's place. Then he had his own pope crown him as Emperor of the Holy Roman Empire.

Meanwhile, by being very careful and very wise and sharing scriptures only when the guardians and the Holy Spirit impressed him it was right, Peter helped many of the sincere Christian priests and students to learn more about the Scriptures and to ask some of the questions he had wondered about too.

While being away from his family was very difficult, the presence of the Most High was with Peter. In all of my experience as a recording angel, I have never seen the Most High's people forsaken. I have seen them lonely and even confused, but the Mighty One has never yet abandoned them, and I am confident he will stay close to Peter too.

EPILOGUE

By the time Peter was an old man, hundreds of people had read the Scripture portions he had secretly shared with them. Now they were following God and boldly preaching the truth as clearly as they understood it. Peter eventually died, but his work did not. Over the years, the Scripture scholars continued to study and share their discoveries with others—including another man named Peter.

The archbishop of Lyons became upset when Peter Waldo criticized the pope and other church leaders. He sent Peter Waldo a message, telling him he should not talk about these things anymore.

Peter sent him back a message. He said, "I cannot be silent in a matter of such importance as the salvation of men's souls. I have to obey God rather than man." The archbishop was furious and went to the newest pope, Alexander III. He excommunicated Peter Waldo and all those who believed his teachings. He told the archbishop of Lyons he could exterminate them. But in spite of terrible persecution, Waldo's followers flourished. They became known as the Waldenses. Many of them moved out of the cities and into the mountains. They lived in caves and valleys just like Peter's family.

The guardians spent a great deal of time with the Waldenses. They were terribly persecuted, and I was sent to England to record the activities of a man named Wycliffe.

JANESSA

ENGLAND AND BOHEMIA, A.D. 1392-1416

y next recording assignment took me to the island of Britain, where I was following a teenage lady-in-waiting named Janessa. She served Queen Anne, young wife of England's King Richard II.

"Uncle Jerome! Uncle Jerome!" Janessa squealed as she ran down the hall toward him.

Uncle Jerome spread his arms and wrapped Janessa in a huge bear hug. Uncle Jerome was a Christian priest and unmarried, but he was like a father to his niece, Janessa.

"How good to see you, Janessa. Life in England must agree with you. You're much taller than the last time I saw you!"

She laughed. "Oh, don't be silly, Uncle Jerome. You always say that!"

"Seriously," Uncle Jerome said, stepping back and looking at her closely, "how are you doing, Janessa?"

Janessa looked down at her shoes. "I miss home," she said. "I love Queen Anne, and we have a lot of fun together, but she is homesick too. Do you think I'll ever get to come home?"

Uncle Jerome shook his head. "I don't know, Janessa," he said. "For now, we have to be thankful for visits we are able to have with each other. We never know what God has planned for our lives."

"Oh, well," sighed Janessa. "Come with me and let me introduce you to the queen."

Later, as they sat talking, Janessa looked over at her friend, the queen. "It's safe," she whispered. "You can tell Uncle Jerome."

The queen raised an eyebrow and then turned to Jerome. "There's a man in this country," she whispered, "who has been raising quite a flap among the church leaders."

"Oh, really?" Uncle Jerome replied. "A heretic?"

"Some think he is," the queen replied slowly. "His name is Wycliffe. He is encouraging people to read the Scriptures for themselves."

"What a novel idea!" Jerome exclaimed.

"Yes," the queen replied. "But as people study the simple, compassionate life of Jesus, they'll see quite a contrast to the lives of many church leaders today."

"I'm sure they will," Jerome remarked grimly.

"Here, let me show you," Queen Anne said. She brought out a book by John Wycliffe and some sheets of paper with scriptures on them.

Janessa, Uncle Jerome, and the queen spent much of their free time together studying Wycliffe's writings. It seemed too soon when Uncle Jerome had to leave to go back to Bohemia.

"I wish you could stay," Janessa cried.

"I know," Uncle Jerome soothed, "but I work for her majesty's brother, King Wenceslas, and I need to go back to his court."

Queen Anne said, "I could write to him and ask if I could have you for my court instead."

Jerome laughed. "Ladies," he said. "I really do need to get home!"

"May I send some of Dr. Wycliffe's writings home with you?" Queen Anne asked.

"Why, certainly," Uncle Jerome replied. "I would be delighted to take them back with me. I would like to see these teachings studied more."

"Oh, so would I," Queen Anne agreed. "I would do anything, just anything, to see this message spread back in my home country."

Uncle Jerome paused. "Would you really do anything at all, even if it meant your death?"

"Anything," said the queen firmly.

"Good for you, your majesty!" Uncle Jerome declared. "Anytime we are willing to do anything, the Lord is able to use us in whatever His plan is."

Uncle Jerome left for Bohemia (known to some of you as the Czech Republic) with some of Wycliffe's writings. As he waved good-bye, he said, "I've had a good time with you. I love you, and I'll miss you. I hope I get to see you both again soon. I can't wait to share these with my friend, John."

BOHEMIA, A.D. 1394

The carriage rattled to a stop in front of Uncle Jerome's house. The door was flung open, and Janessa was scooped out and then placed in Uncle Jerome's strong arms.

"Janessa," he said quietly as he looked down into her puffy, swollen eyes. Janessa wrapped her arms around Uncle Jerome's neck and burst into tears.

"It was so awful, Uncle Jerome!" she cried. "What am I going to do now?"

"You are going to come inside and get warm, and then you can tell me all about it," he replied. "You can live here with me until you get married . . ."

"I'm *never* getting married!" she sobbed determinedly.

"Well, I'm not either," he reminded her. "You can live here with me until I turn into an old coot, and you'll still be young enough to take care of me," he joked.

"Oh, Uncle Jerome! Could I? Please?" she begged.

"Of course!" he replied. "Now come in and get warm."

She paused. "Oh. My luggage."

"Here are your trunks, ma'am," the burly coachman said, gesturing to four large pieces of luggage sitting behind the coach.

"You certainly came home with a lot more than you took with you," Uncle Jerome observed. "The queen must have been very good to you."

"Yes," Janessa sniffed. "She was."

Uncle Jerome tried to pick up one trunk and stopped. "What on earth do you have in these?" he asked. "Bars of lead? Large English rocks? Some of that heavy English cooking?"

Janessa giggled in spite of her tears. "I didn't bring back a stitch of clothing or any of that fancy stuff," she said.

Soon they were inside Uncle Jerome's house, and Janessa unlocked the trunks. They were filled with books.

"What are these?" Uncle Jerome asked.

"These are all of Her Majesty's books," replied Janessa. "She wanted you to have them. She wants Dr. Wycliffe's teachings to be shared with the people here in her country."

"So she knew she was dying?" Uncle Jerome asked.

"Yes. She got sick so fast, but she had time and the clearness of mind to think of you. The other ladies think she was poisoned."

"Shhh!" Uncle Jerome said as he dropped his voice to a whisper. "It is never safe to share those suspicions out loud, even when you are almost certain you are alone. Even the walls have ears these days."

Janessa dropped her voice and whispered to Uncle Jerome. "She and the king did not agree on religion. He was a very unkind man. The queen was only a little older than I am. It was just awful!"

Uncle Jerome wrapped his arms around his little niece. "I am so glad you are back here where it is safe," he whispered. He closed his eyes, offering thanks to God.

I shuddered. Did her uncle really think it was safer in Bohemia? Was there any place on this sinful little planet that could be considered safe? I shook my head. Fortunately, neither of the tearful humans could see me.

"Janessa," Uncle Jerome said as he finished supper. "This has been a terrible experience for you, but it could have been an answer to prayers."

"Whose?" Janessa asked sarcastically. "King Richard's?"

"No," Uncle Jerome replied slowly. "Anne's."

"How?" his niece demanded between bites.

"Remember when I visited you in England?"

Janessa nodded, chewing slowly.

"Remember when Anne said she would be willing to do anything, even if it cost her life, to share these teachings with her people in Bohemia?"

"Oh," Janessa said. "She did say that. Now all her books are here in her home country. Do you think this is the way God answered her? I could feel much better about all this if I thought that Anne was willing to give her life to help her people learn more about God. That is much easier to live with than just remembering how miserably she was treated and how I think she might have died. It was such an ugly way to die."

I smiled at the guardians. They were smiling too. If these poor humans could just see what we see, they would never choose any plan other than the one the Almighty has given them. If only they could know that, no matter what happened, He is still King of the universe, and His plans would still go forward. Of course, they had been told this in the Scriptures, but humans are quite forgetful. Still, the Mighty One's Spirit often whooshes in and shares His plans with them, deep inside their thoughts.

I knew that if Janessa could remember this experience, she would be a strong warrior in the continuing battle. After seeing life with Queen Anne and her husband, she may never want to marry, but she need not be married to do the job the Almighty has in mind.

MEGAN: TOWER OF LONDON, A.D. 1401

I returned to the island the natives call England to record the choices of Megan, a little girl who lived in London. Megan was still a child, only 10 years old by human count, and from a very poor family. She had been given a job in the Tower of London as a scullery maid. Though she was paid very little, she was fed in the tower kitchens and was able to take a little money home to her family.

I followed her as she struggled up the cold stone stairs lugging a huge bucket of coal. The burly jailer stomped along ahead of her, his keys jangling with each step. Reaching a large door, he unlocked it and said, "Knock when you're done and ready to come out." Timidly she stepped into the room, and he locked the door behind her. She seemed to be unaware of the guardians with her and looked very frightened. The rooms were not well lit, and it took her a few moments for her eyes to adjust.

"I'm not going to bite you," said a deep voice in the corner. She jumped. The man laughed. "Come over here where I can see you."

Megan walked timidly toward the light spilling in from a grate high in the wall. The man was in the darkest corner of the room, and she could see nothing but shadows.

"Poor child—you're shaking. Are you frightened?"

Megan didn't answer.

"Ah, you are wondering what kind of criminal I am, and whether I'm going to hurt you?"

Megan nodded shyly, staring at the floor.

"Well, you can relax. I haven't killed anyone, nor do I intend to any time in the future. I don't hurt women, and I certainly never pick on children."

"But, then, why are you here?" Megan blurted before she could stop herself. "If you are not a violent criminal, then you must have plotted against the king."

The man's laugh boomed through the stone room again. Whoever he was, he had a sense of humor and an infectious laugh. "I never plotted against my king," he said seriously. "The king and I are friends." He stepped out from the shadows and into the light.

"Oh, my Lord Cobham!" Megan whispered, sinking to her knees.

"Oh, get up," Lord Cobham said. "I don't think you need to kneel to me in here."

"What happened to you?" Megan asked. "Why are you in here? Surely the king will have you out of here in no time. It must be a mistake."

"It is no mistake," replied Lord Cobham grimly. "Have you heard of Dr. Wycliffe?"

"Just that he is a terrible heretic and that his followers are those Lollards, who have a funny accent and aren't too smart. We were laughing at some in the square just the other day. My brothers were following them through the town swaying back and forth and imitating their funny hymns but adding naughty words to them. I hadn't had so much fun in I don't know how long! But I don't know anything about the doctor. Why do you ask?"

"Well, I am in here for being one of those not-too-smart people."

"Oh! My lord! Forgive me!" Megan cried, falling on her knees again. "Please don't have me beaten. I didn't know. I . . ."

"Get up! Get up!" Lord Cobham barked irritably. "Nobody is going to beat you. Considering that I am a prisoner here, I doubt if anyone cares what you say to me. Besides, I believe it is customary to be rude to prisoners in the tower," he added with a twinkle.

"Do you ever read the Scriptures?" he asked, changing the subject.

"I go to mass every Sunday—well, er, most Sundays—and the priest reads us the mass," she replied.

Lord Cobham persisted, "But have *you* ever read them?"

"I go to mass, and I cross myself and do whatever the priest tells me to," she persisted defensively. "Of course I don't read it myself—it's in Latin."

"What if you could get part of the Scriptures in English?" Lord Cobham asked patiently.

Megan twisted her apron. "It wouldn't do me much good," she answered softly. "I can't read English neither."

"Of course, forgive me," Lord Cobham apologized. "You've probably never been given a chance to learn to read."

"No, my lord, but I'm pretty bright, and I learn as fast as a boy. If it ever was to happen, I'd be reading everything in sight in no time, I would!"

"I'll make you a deal," the man offered. "Life in the tower is pretty lonely, at least in the prison part." They both laughed, knowing that on the other side the tower royal apartments were where King Henry and his court stayed—and partied.

"If you will come and spend some time with me each day after you finish your tasks, I will teach you to read. I promise to be absolutely respectable, and if you are unhappy or afraid at any time, you can just knock on the door, and the jailer will let you leave."

While this would have been a foolish deal to make with most criminals in the tower, Megan was falling right into a plan the

Most High had for her life. I already knew what the brave Lord Cobham would use for reading materials to teach Megan. For a recording job in a prison, this was going to be fun!

* * *

"Tell me more about Dr. Wycliffe," Megan requested as she entered Lord Cobham's cell with his lunch. "Is he a doctor who helped sick people?"

Lord Cobham shook his head. "No, he was called Dr. Wycliffe because he was a professor at the University of Oxford. He was a very serious Bible student."

"Ah," she replied. "So he was just a doctor for people who were sick of sin."

Lord Cobham laughed. "You have that right," he said. "As he translated the Scriptures and shared them with his students and others, he found things that were different than the church leaders were teaching. He felt that many church leaders were lazy, taking money from poor people but not helping the people whom they accepted money from. Dr. Wycliffe believed they should use the money to help the sick and the poor and those who had nothing, as Jesus did. If Jesus were their example, then they should be helping people and not just getting rich off the poor people."

"Well, that makes sense," commented Megan.

"There was more," Lord Cobham continued. "As he studied and translated, Dr. Wycliffe found that the Scriptures teach that God's plan of salvation is enough for us to be saved. We don't have to have a lot of extra rules, and we don't have to go through priests and popes to beg God to save us. He already loved us and made a plan to save us. What Jesus did for us was enough."

This sounded very strange and new to Megan. I watched her chew her lip thoughtfully before answering.

"I guess that makes sense too. If He is the king of the universe, then He's strong enough and powerful enough to save us all by Himself. He wouldn't need us to go through other weak humans who make mistakes."

I smiled. This girl had a tender heart combined with an open mind and willingness to learn.

Lord Cobham nodded. "And Dr. Wycliffe taught that forcing people to keep lots of extra rules wouldn't help them be any more saved or any more acceptable to God."

"No wonder the church leaders hated him," Megan said. "It sounds as if they were mad at him just because if everyone believed the way Dr. Wycliffe taught, they would not be as powerful."

"You're right," Lord Cobham replied.

"Did they kill him?" she asked.

Lord Cobham laughed. "No! They hated him, all right, but he was a friend of King Edward."

"Edward III?"

"Yes," answered the young lord. "You know your kings. Dr. Wycliffe became chaplain to the king."

"You mean like the king's personal pastor?" she asked.

"Yes. He and King Edward were very good friends."

"Kind of like you and King Henry?"

Lord Cobham nodded. "Yes, kind of like King Henry and me. For a while they convinced King Edward to send Dr. Wycliffe as an ambassador to the Netherlands, but after two years he was back. They wanted very badly to get rid of him and even tried to take him to court for heresy, but the judges were too afraid to convict him, so they let him go."

"You are a friend of the king too," Megan began. "But you are locked up here in the tower."

"Yes," Lord Cobham answered.

"Why?" she asked. "Why doesn't King Henry protect you?"

"Shhh! It is very important never to say anything that could sound disloyal to our God or our king."

"Even if he lets you be put in jail?" Megan asked.

"Right," Lord Cobham answered. "Even if he lets you be put in jail. We don't always understand what God has in mind when He allows things to happen, but we need to never be disloyal to Him. King Henry is my friend, and I am not disloyal to him either."

"I don't understand," Megan murmured.

"Well," Lord Cobham replied, "you know we have had two kings who did not reign very long, and there has been a lot of unrest in our country."

"Yes," she answered. "Kings Richard II and Henry. Neither one of them had long reigns like Edward's."

"Right," said Lord Cobham. "King Henry is the king, but he understands how shaky his position is. He needs to maintain the support of the church leaders because they are so powerful."

"And so because you are a follower of Dr. Wycliffe, they hate you and want you put in jail?"

"Yes. The king has protected me many times before, but right now he is needing to protect himself."

"But . . . but . . . ," Megan protested.

Lord Cobham smiled. "Each one of us faces a time in our life when our loyalty to God is tested. Mine is now, and I choose to be loyal to God and what I believe He wants me to do. Right now King Henry is choosing to protect himself, and I understand that. You too, Megan, will have to choose which side you'll be on. At some point you will be brought to a crossroads where you will have to choose whether you will follow God or other people's ideas."

I nodded in agreement, even though neither of them could see me. All humans must make this choice at some time in their lives.

Megan looked at her feet. It all sounded so difficult. She wasn't sure that she could follow God if they were going to put her in a cell in the tower as they had done to Lord Cobham.

"Megan, don't look so afraid," he said. "When the time comes, the Lord gives you all the courage you need. He gives us everything we need when we need it. Don't be afraid. Just learn what you can about Him now."

She smiled.

Lord Cobham said, "I'm going to eat my lunch now that it's nice and cold."

Megan giggled. "I'm sorry," she said, "but thank you for telling me more about Dr. Wycliffe."

* * *

I watched with interest as the friendship between Megan and Lord Cobham deepened and developed. Megan was a bright girl and learned to read quickly. Lord Cobham shared small portions of Scripture with her that she took home and shared with her very large family. Soon several friends were gathering in her home in the evenings to hear the Scripture portions that she brought home. The Almighty's plan was going well.

One day Megan was very troubled.

"What's the matter, child?" Lord Cobham asked as she entered his cell. "You are so quiet today."

Megan burst into tears.

"Come now," he said. "It can't be that bad."

"It is," she snuffled, wiping her nose on her sleeve. "I heard some gossip down in the courtyard today. They say you might be executed."

Lord Cobham was quiet.

"Is it true?" she demanded. "Have you heard?"

"No," he said, "I haven't been told anything, but that is always a possibility. Not too long ago Parliament put through a bill that made it legal to burn people who teach things different than the church leaders teach. So it is possible, because I do."

Megan sobbed. "But that would be terrible!"

"Well, it certainly wouldn't be my first choice," Lord Cobham answered, "but that does sometimes happen, and I knew that was a possibility when I made these choices."

Megan stopped crying and stared at him. "But you're a friend of the king. Would he let that happen?"

"I don't know," Lord Cobham said thoughtfully. Then he asked, "If I write a letter, will you take it to a friend of mine?"

"I'll do anything to help you," Megan answered. "You know I will."

"I'll work on it tomorrow," Lord Cobham replied, "and when you bring me my lunch, I'll place it under the bowl on the tray when you take it away."

Megan nodded. "I'll do whatever it takes to get you out of here."

It made me sad to see Megan so worried. I knew that though King Henry was sympathetic toward Lord Cobham and felt guilty about his imprisonment, he would not read the letter. He was too weak to stand up to the powerful leaders who opposed Wycliffe's teachings.

"Have you heard anything back from the king?" Megan asked a few days later.

"Nothing," replied Lord Cobham. "He may not feel he is able to help me right now."

"What is going to happen?" Megan asked, twisting her apron nervously.

"We must not panic," Lord Cobham said. "We must pray about it, and if the Lord gives us a way of escape, we must take it. But if He doesn't, then we must face whatever the plan is, bravely, and trust Him."

Megan's eyes widened as she watched him. I could see it all sinking into her mind. Then she asked, "How did Dr. Wycliffe die?"

"Ah, that's a lovely story," Lord Cobham answered. "He got very ill one time. The church leaders who had been his enemies were delighted. All of them gathered around his bedside and told him he was dying. Gasping for breath, Dr. Wycliffe told them, 'I shall not die but live and declare the glory of the Lord.'"

"They all went away shaking their heads in disgust," Lord Cobham continued. "Sure enough, Dr. Wycliffe got better and went on translating the New Testament and teaching people about God's love for them. Three more times they tried to take him to court and accuse him of heresy, and three more times the judges refused to find him guilty, and he was set free."

"So he died an old man?" Megan asked.

"Yes," Lord Cobham replied. "Fifty-four is pretty old, don't you think?"

"Ah, yes," Megan said. "Fifty-four is very old! Most people don't live nearly that long here."

Lord Cobham smiled. "Although all of us would like to," he said. Megan laughed. "Dr. Wycliffe was in his church worshiping God and was just about to start the Communion service when he died suddenly."

"How terrible!" exclaimed Megan.

"No," Lord Cobham said. "It wasn't. Right before we participate in Communion, we pray and ask our Lord to clear our hearts of anything wrong. It was the perfect time to die. His heart was right with Jesus, and there was nothing to separate them."

"Oh," Megan said slowly, "then I guess that was a good time after all."

"Yes, it was," Lord Cobham replied. "And if I should be executed here in the tower, it will be just like that because I will already know when I am going to die. I've already confessed all my sins, and there is nothing to separate me from the love of Jesus either. And if that should happen, it is going to be OK. I am not afraid. Whenever it happens, it will be a good time."

I hoped that these thoughts lodged firmly in Megan's mind. She would need to remember them later.

EPILOGUE

Later that year, after cautioning Megan to be careful of false doctrines and always to search the Scriptures and find out the truth, Lord Cobham escaped from the tower. Megan missed him terribly, but she was glad he had escaped. It was part of the plan of the Almighty for him to share these things with her—and with others in Europe.

In December of the human year A.D. 1417, he returned from France and hid himself with a friend, Lord Powis, in his castle in Wales. But Lord Powis was not the friend Lord Cobham thought him to be. He turned Lord Cobham over to his enemies in England. Lord Cobham was hanged, then burned on the scaffold.

How carefully the Mighty One had prepared Megan for this time. The things that Lord Cobham taught her came back to her mind. She continued to work in the tower and faced the sad day with great bravery.

During this time, many followers of Dr. Wycliffe died for their faith, but as more died, even more sprang up, such as Megan and her family. Nothing humans did could stop the Mighty One's plans.

I smiled as I continued to record.

JEROME'S HOME: BOHEMIA, A.D. 1415

Janessa lifted the heavy crock of soup onto the table and passed around a platter of dark rye bread. Uncle Jerome smiled at her. "I'm afraid, Janessa, that this isn't the kind of rich food you're used to."

Janessa laughed. "Uncle Jerome, I would much rather eat simple food and be home with you. I was very homesick in the palace." Everyone laughed, and then they bowed their heads for grace.

Uncle Jerome had some friends over for dinner. One of them

was his friend John, whom he had mentioned to Queen Anne. Janessa learned that John was actually Professor Huss, the dean and rector of Prague University. He had read everything Uncle Jerome had given him and had proceeded to teach Dr. Wycliffe's writings to all of his students. Now he was helping to distribute the books that Queen Anne had sent back after her death.

The church leaders were very angry about it and had told Professor Huss he could not teach these things anymore. "So what are we going to do?" one friend asked.

"I shall continue doing what I have been doing," Professor Huss said.

Uncle Jerome nodded. The other two friends were not so sure. "If they've told us that we cannot preach these things anymore, then we could lose our jobs. You have a very important one at the university, but Eric and I are just common laborers. They could kill us without causing any notice at all."

Professor Huss looked at them quietly. "The Lord will tell each of us what He wants us to do, but for now I feel that the Lord wants me to continue teaching."

The two friends looked at each other. The conversation continued late into the night. Janessa sat listening quietly and drawing little pictures in the sawdust on the floor.

Suddenly one of Uncle Jerome's friends jumped up. "I've got it," he cried. "We can obey the commands of our rulers and still do what God wants us to do."

"But how?" Janessa asked.

"We need ingredients to make pigments and paint. Both of us are artistic. We can do artwork in public places. We won't say a word because it is preaching that we're not allowed to do."

"This sounds interesting," Janessa said. "I'll help you."

The following day Janessa helped them get everything they needed: paintbrushes, oils, and pigments. Soon they were set up in the town center. They started painting. One of them painted a picture of Jesus riding into Jerusalem. He was dressed very simply and was meekly sitting on the back of a donkey. His disciples were with Him in their simple clothing and bare feet.

The other picture portrayed a magnificent procession led by the pope in his rich robes and triple crown mounted on a horse with gold all over its bridle and saddle. He was proceeded by trumpeters and followed by cardinals in their flashy red robes decorated everywhere with gold and jewels. Though neither artist said a word, everyone looking at the pictures could see the tremendous contrast between the two.

This was what Dr. Wycliffe had been preaching about. This was what Dr. Huss had been teaching about at the university. The whole sermon was in a picture, and the two men had not said a word!

Janessa clapped her hands in delight. *How good God is!* she thought to herself. *He gives us a way around any obstacle so that we can still do what pleases Him.*

I drew close. I wanted Janessa to remember this thought for some of the hard times that would come ahead. In the huge battle between good and evil, even God's children go through very difficult times. It would be important for her to remember these things.

* * *

"I don't want you to go, Professor Huss," Janessa explained. "It's too dangerous, and you have many enemies now."

Professor Huss laughed. "Don't be afraid, Janessa," he said. "Look how the Lord has taken care of me so far. The bishops were angry with me and wanted to take me to trial in Rome, but the king and queen protected me. They had to have the trial without me, and they sentenced without me. They weren't able to figure out how to have an execution without me, so they skipped that part."

They all laughed. "Yes," Uncle Jerome said, "God has been good to us, but Janessa is right. There are great dangers out there."

"Well," Professor Huss said, "Emperor Sigismund has promised to give me safe passage to appear before the council in Constance. The emperor himself is going to be there. I trust him, and who would dare disobey his promise?"

They all looked at each other. "We will pray for your safety," Uncle Jerome said.

"I will go with you," Janessa said. "You need somebody to come along and take care of you."

After some protesting, Janessa got her wish. Later, she wrote back to Uncle Jerome from Constance.

"It was amazing, Uncle Jerome. It was just like those pictures Professor Huss's friends painted. When the emperor arrived in Constance, there were more than 100,000 foreigners in the city. Some 36,000 beds were set up for people still coming, and there are at least 30,000 horses in the city.

"The pope is here, and he brought 600 people. The emperor brought 4,000 people. There are 30 cardinals here, four patriarchs, and two of the pope's legates, and each of them has a whole herd of attendants.

"There are 27 archbishops, 206 bishops, 33 titular bishops, 150 other important people, and 203 abbots. And each of them has a whole herd of people taking care of them too. The city is just packed with all these pompous people and their bodyguards, and their servants, and the servants of their servants, and the servants of their servants of their servants. Fine clothes and jewels are everywhere.

"Then came Professor Huss with me and his two friends, walking and carrying our few belongings with us. You would have laughed. It was just like the paintings.

"More later.

"Love,

"Janessa."

CONSTANCE, BADEN-WÜRTTEMBERG: A.D. 1415

The guardians and I drew close to Janessa and her little band. All day we reminded them how God had taken care of them in the past. We knew they would need to remember these things very soon.

Suddenly there was a crash, and the door flew open. Soldiers poured into the room. Professor Huss stood. "Gentlemen," he said, "what is the meaning of this?"

"You're under arrest," one of the soldiers replied.

"That can't be!" Professor Huss protested. "I have a promise of safe passage from my king. I have it in writing."

The soldier glanced at the paper and then flung it on the floor. "Yes," he said, "Emperor Sigismund may have promised that, but the pope didn't. We're here on his orders, and you are in big trouble."

"Ah," Professor Huss said, a look of understanding dawning across his face. He said nothing else. Janessa shook silently as they led him away. She was too numb to cry. She followed at a safe distance to see where they would take him.

"I will find out information," she whispered to the other followers, "if there is a way for me to visit him and take him food." However, when she got to the jail, she was turned away at the door.

"No visitors allowed to heretics," the guard growled.

"Will they feed him?" she asked, knowing that many people in prison didn't eat unless family or friends brought them food.

"It doesn't matter," laughed another soldier. "Go away and forget about this."

Janessa paled, but she set her chin firmly. She determined in her heart that every time the shift changed and there were new guards, she would request to visit Professor Huss and see if someone would let her in.

* * *

Janessa returned to their rented rooms and slumped in a chair, exhausted. It had been three days since Professor Huss had been arrested. The jailers would still not allow her to visit him. The two friends who had traveled there with her and Professor Huss would be home soon. She started to make a fire in the fireplace. The door opened, and she sprang to her feet.

"What did you find out?" she asked.

"Nothing yet," one said grimly as he turned to the other. "We must draw up a petition at least. We must ask for him to be released on bail, or he will die before he ever gets to trial in that prison. Word has it that he is not being fed."

Janessa sank back into her chair. The two men pored over their petition all evening and had it ready to present to the courts in the morning. The petition was presented to the council the next day, signed by several of the most distinguished noblemen in Bohemia. The court considered it and sent four bishops and two lords to the prison to try to talk Professor Huss into recanting his position.

"He won't recant," Janessa said. "I know he won't. He believes what God said in the Scriptures. He won't back down now."

The noblemen shook their heads hopelessly. "I think we should watch the streets," they said. "If he does not recant, they plan to bring him before the court and the emperor. We may be able to see him as he goes by."

The guardians and I pulled in close, trying to infuse the little group of believers with as much strength as we could for what they were about to face. Sure enough, Professor Huss was brought from the council. Janessa looked at the ground. She couldn't even bear to look at him. They had stripped him of his priest's robe he usually wore when teaching. To degrade and embarrass him they put a paper crown on his head with devils painted all over it and a sign that said, "Ringleader of heretics."

Professor Huss, however, walked with great dignity. He held his head high and looked almost joyful. He was paraded through the streets to the emperor, who sent him on to the duke.

The crowds followed in the streets to see what would happen next. There seemed to be a gathering at the gates of the church. Janessa stood on the edge of the little wall to try to see what was happening. There people were throwing books in front of the gate. She realized they were books Professor Huss had written.

Suddenly there was a puff of smoke and a cheer from the crowd. They were burning his books. *At least they're not burning him,* she thought. The procession moved on to the edge of town. A stake was fastened into the ground with chains and piles of wood next to it. Janessa's heart sank. "O God," she prayed silently, "aren't You going to save him? Won't You save my professor? Please help him."

Professor Huss looked over at Janessa. He smiled and looked very relaxed. The soldiers grabbed the rusty chain and wrapped it around him, securing him to the stake. "Jesus was bound with worse chains than this for my sake," he said. "Why should I be ashamed of this little rusty one?"

Janessa understood. Professor Huss was going to die. If she was going to help, it would be to help him die bravely. She pushed toward the front of the crowd and smiled at him. He smiled back at her. Professor Huss said softly, "Jesus was wrapped in a robe that wasn't His when He was on trial. They took away His clothes too. Jesus wore a crown of thorns for me. I can wear this dunce cap for Him." He continued to smile and looked very calm as they piled the wood around his feet. Then they lit the fire. Instead of screaming, Professor Huss began to sing.

Janessa started to pray. "O God, please help him to be brave. Please help him not to hurt." Huss sang louder and louder. The higher the flames went, the higher his song went, until all was quiet.

Janessa fell to her knees. "Oh, thank You, Jesus," she whispered. If the professor had been able to sing clear to the end, that meant God had given him extra courage and had stopped the pain enough so that he could sing praises. "You are so good," she continued. "Just wait till I tell Uncle Jerome."

* * *

Almost a year had passed. Janessa had been taken in by a noble family when her uncle Jerome was arrested. Even though the emperor had promised safety to Professor Huss, he had not stood up to the pope and the council in the end. Now Uncle Jerome was in their power too. He had been in prison for 340 days. Janessa's spirits were good; the guardians had strengthened her, and her loyalty was unshaken.

"O God," she prayed before learning of Uncle Jerome's trial. "You know many of Your enemies are pretending to be friends of Yours, and yet they are just trying to build up their own power and kill anybody who gets in their way. Please be with my uncle Jerome. If there is any way to save him, please do that. But if he is to die, please help him to be brave, as our friend the professor was. And God, please help him not to hurt. I love him so much."

Janessa looked peaceful as she got up from her knees and joined the line in the streets with the others who were waiting to see what had happened. Before long a roar came over the crowd. Uncle Jerome was being dragged from the council chamber. He was wearing the same big paper cap painted with red devils.

Uncle Jerome stopped and spoke, "Our Lord Jesus Christ, when He suffered death for me, a most miserable sinner, wore a crown of thorns on His head, and I, for His sake, will wear this cap."

The cardinal of Florence tried again to talk him into giving up his beliefs and cooperating with the powerful leaders. Jerome said no and began to sing. Janessa smiled. *He knows how comforting it was to me that Professor Huss sang clear to the end. It's Uncle Jerome's way of letting me know God is giving him courage!*

Uncle Jerome sang all the way to the spot where Professor Huss had been burned. Then he knelt down and prayed.

The crowd was silent as they listened for each word, then he hugged the stake cheerfully, and the soldiers fastened him to it. Janessa's stomach hurt, but she kept her chin up bravely as she watched, for the Lord was answering her prayers and making Uncle Jerome brave.

As the executioner sneaked up behind to light the wood, Uncle Jerome said, "Come around to the front. You can light it in front of me, for if I were afraid of this, I would never have come here to Constance."

The fire was lit, and Uncle Jerome began to sing again. There was no screaming and no crying. The last words he sang were "This soul in flames, I offer, Christ, to Thee."

Janessa was shaking, and her fists were clenched, but she was proud of Uncle Jerome, and she was proud of her God, who could get His people through the worst executions without a cry of pain. God had answered her prayer, and she knew, without a doubt, she would serve Him as long as she lived.

M'ax

ax gasped in shock. Could he have heard correctly? Timidly he raised his hand. "Professor Luther, would you repeat that one more time, please?"

Professor Luther looked at him and smiled. "I said," he repeated, "that I myself have heard people say openly in the streets of Rome, 'If there be a hell, Rome is built on it.'"

Max had heard correctly. Professor Luther was his favorite teacher at the University of Wittenberg. He was a priest from the Augustinian monastery there in Wittenberg. He had very strong opinions and could be harsh sometimes, but he was no harder on his students than he was on himself. And he liked Max. Max's full name was Maximilian Schlossburg. His friends called him Max, but Professor Luther had nicknamed him "Minim" his first day in class.

"A lad your size isn't big enough to be called Max yet," he said with a twinkle. He and Professor Luther had become good friends from that day on.

Another student raised his hand. "Professor Luther, are you saying that you believe our church is corrupt?"

Professor Luther took a deep breath and sighed. "There are

things in our church," he began, "that do not reflect the teachings that I have studied from the Word of God. However, few of us ever get to read the sacred words or study them for ourselves, so we are dependent on the way it is taught to us by our church leaders. I believe that some things have been changed to benefit the church leaders rather than the church or God Himself."

"Professor Luther, can you give us an example of this?" asked one of the students.

"Certainly," replied the professor. "Consider our church headquarters . . ."

"The Vatican?" asked Max.

"Yes," answered Luther. "Saint Peter's is about 1,200 years old now and in need of repairs. Every loyal Christian in Europe would admit that our church headquarters should be a place of beauty and should be kept in good repair. However, our present pope, Leo X, has plans to make of it a grand palace such as has never been seen in Europe. In fact, the design for the dome is so grandiose that the architects are not even sure how they're going to get it to stay up. They're still working on that one."

"How is he going to pay for all this?" the professor continued. "The donations people are making to the church are already being used for other things, so our leadership had to come up with another way to finance this huge building project. The solution to this problem is the concept of indulgences."

Several of the students nodded. They had heard about indulgences.

"Yes," Luther said, "it is possible to pay a sum of money and receive an indulgence from God through your local priest or indulgence seller, no matter what the sin was. This money goes directly into the building project."

"It sounds like a good idea," one student suggested. "I would think they would get a lot of money that way."

Professor Luther nodded. "Ah, yes, that they will. However, the Scriptures tell us very plainly that the Son of God died for our sins and that by faith in Him alone we are forgiven. So scripturally there is no foundation for paying large amounts of money to our church for forgiveness when we can get it free for the asking directly from God."

Maximilian raised his hand. "Minim," Luther responded.

"Professor, does that mean that if we can get forgiveness for sins by paying enough money, it would be possible to buy indulgences in advance for a sin we are planning to commit?"

Professor Luther started to laugh. "The workings of a not-quite-sanctified mind," he mused. "I don't know. That would be a very good question to ask. The pope's representative, who is administering this plan, is in the area this week. His name is John Tetzel. Why don't you go ask him?"

Several of the boys nodded. "We will, sir, and we'll bring you back his answer."

I started to chuckle as I followed Maximilian and his friends out of the classroom. Tetzel should have seen this coming a long time ago. The rowdy boys chatted about their plans all through supper.

"We could buy indulgences now while they're cheap, before they catch on and get expensive," one said, "and we could save them up and use them for whenever we wanted to cheat in class or do something else."

"Let's ask first," another replied. "If we can really buy indulgences before committing a sin, why not buy all the indulgences we need for the next year and then commit the sin of robbery and steal all our money back from Tetzel?"

The boys roared with laughter. "What a wonderful idea!" they said.

The first boy added, "And if God didn't invent the idea of indulgences anyway, do you think He would mind if we beat up Tetzel?"

Maximilian felt uncomfortable. He didn't think that stealing was right under any circumstances, whether you were stealing from God or not.

After dinner the boys trouped out into the village square and started asking around, "Have you seen Tetzel from Rome?" They soon found him.

"Of course," Tetzel said smoothly. "I see no problem with buying your indulgences in advance, especially since I'm not sure how long I'll be here in town. You're obviously sons of wealthy families who can afford to purchase your indulgences in advance."

Maximilian's stomach felt worse, but he said nothing. Several of the boys passed over their money to Tetzel, who wrote out their indulgences carefully on small pieces of parchment.

"Keep track of these," he said, "and when you go to confession, just surrender them to your priest, and you will be absolved of any sins you may commit for the next year."

"Thank you, Father Tetzel. That's wonderful," said the last boy as he pocketed his indulgence. Then the bigger boys pounced on Tetzel.

"Wait, wait, what are you doing, you bad boys?" he shouted. "You'll burn in hell for this!"

"No, we won't. We have indulgences!"

Maximilian crept behind a tree and watched. He felt as guilty as if he were stealing from Tetzel, too, even though he was just watching. Should he tell Professor Luther?

* * *

Professor Luther frowned at his classroom full of restless boys. "I understand from a reliable source," he began, "that some of you paid a visit to Tetzel, as we discussed in class yesterday."

Some of the boys snickered and nodded. Others just looked at their feet.

"I received a visit from Tetzel and his entourage last night. Apparently you were testing the validity of the indulgences that you purchased from him. For those of you who believe in the spiritual authority of the indulgences, you are apparently absolved of this sin."

His eyes twinkled, though his face remained grave. "However, those of you who wish to base your lives on the Scriptures and what God really said will recall that He did say, 'Thou shalt not steal.' Beating up Tetzel was not a very Christian thing to do. I don't wish to hear of this happening again, and especially not in my name. Is that understood clearly?" The boys nodded.

Professor Luther began to crack a smile as he continued: "It is fortunate for you boys that the Lord offered another way for you to be absolved of your sins, since Tetzel will probably not be interested in selling you particular people any more indulgences. Now let's turn to our lesson for today."

Max's stomach had been upset ever since the run-in with Tetzel. He decided to talk to Professor Luther after the class.

I stayed with Max, as I was assigned. However, I noticed large groups of guardians clustering wherever Professor Luther went. Guardians also accompanied Maximilian and me and many of the other students in Professor Luther's classes.

Later that evening there was a knock on Professor Luther's cell door. Maximilian entered Professor Luther's cell. It was very bare. There was just a bed in one corner and a cross on the wall, and it was cold.

"Is this is where you sleep?" Max asked.

"Yes, Minim," Professor Luther answered. "A priest like me doesn't need very much. I have a bed on which to sleep, a floor on which to kneel and pray, a cross on the wall to remind me of Jesus, and a window to let in this wonderful fresh air."

"Brr," Max remarked. "It lets in way too much this time of year."

Professor Luther chuckled. "Yes, it is brisk this evening. What's on your mind, Minim?"

Max paused for a moment and then spelled out his confession. Professor Luther laughed. "It sounds like you saw Tetzel receive the logical conclusion of his great idea," he said. "However, I am glad that you were not involved in the violence."

"But was I wrong?" asked Maximilian. "Was this a sin?"

Professor Luther leaned back against the wall, then shut his eyes for a moment. "I guess violence is always wrong," he said. "However, there are a good many times when I feel pretty violent myself and have to keep confessing it to the Lord and asking Him to give me a more Christlike nature. There are times when I would like to do some pretty bad things to some of the pompous people who rank higher than I in this organization."

I nodded to myself, knowing that this was a character flaw Professor Luther struggled with. How grateful these humans should be that the Mighty One chooses to use flawed human beings, or no human would ever have a chance at being part of His plan. So far all the humans that I have observed have had character defects. Still, I knew the power of the Holy Spirit, for I had seen Him transform bickering fishermen into powerful preachers. And I knew that the Lord could help Professor Luther to clarify his thinking too.

"There are just so many things," the professor continued after some quiet thought. "I am just quite frustrated."

"Why don't you make a list?" Max asked.

"A list of everything that's frustrating me?" Luther said. "Please—there are only 24 hours in a day."

"No, I'm serious," Max replied. "You could make copies of it and let us discuss them in class."

"Then it would just get back to the higher-ups, and I would be in even more hot water than I am now," Professor Luther said.

Maximilian laughed. "Well, they have their spies everywhere. They always know what you've said in class, because you always get in trouble for it later anyway. Why not just nail it to the door of the cathedral in Wittenberg?"

Maximilian and Luther convulsed with laughter. "Yeah, wouldn't that be great? That would really cause a ruckus here in town. Tetzel thinks he was upset about being robbed; imagine what he would think if I posted my list of frustrations and everything else that is wrong with the church!"

Late that night, after the laughing stopped and Luther spent his hours in prayer, as was his habit, I watched him staring into the darkness, thinking. While I knew that Maximilian had been joking, the professor was getting that determined jut to his chin that I was beginning to associate with events that required many guardians.

Was this priest really going to nail a list of complaints to the door of the cathedral? The Almighty is able to see into the future, though those of us working for Him are not. Sometimes He tells us what's going to happen, and sometimes we just have to watch. But as the guardians continued to cluster, I was almost sure that Maximilian's joke was going to go down in history as a major event.

* * *

A loud thumping outside the door of Wittenberg Cathedral was the noisy ending of a tumultuous day. October 31 often saw celebrations of the most unholy sort, dating back to shortly after Noah's flood. Apparently humans are fairly slow learners. But tonight, in addition to pagan Halloween festivities, church leadership would be infuriated to the very top, and loyal Christians would be confused and have to rethink their stand on many issues. I smiled as I imagined what Maximilian would think when he found out that Professor Luther had worked all day writing his 95 theses—statements about what was wrong with the church.

Early that evening Max crept into the monastery, intending to go to the chapel and pray for Professor Luther. As he turned to enter the small candle-lit chapel he saw the shadow of someone disappearing down the hall. Creeping along quietly, he followed the person out into the courtyard and toward the cathedral. Who would be sneaking around the monastery? The shadow approached the large door and instead of opening it, unrolled several large parchments and began pounding.

"Professor Luther," Maximilian exclaimed in a whisper. "What on earth are you doing?"

"It's my list," Luther said as he continued to nail it to the door.

"You're going to get into much trouble for this!"

Professor Luther paused and glanced at Max. "Yes, I imagine so," he said, and then resumed his pounding.

Max was horrified and delighted, all rolled into one. "Professor Luther," he cried breathlessly, "I can't believe you really did that!"

Professor Luther smiled grimly. "It was a good idea," he said.

"But . . . but . . ." Max protested, "you're going to be in terrible trouble now. You know that Tetzel already hates you. Now everyone up to the Holy Father will hate you too, or at least be pretty mad at you."

"Yes," Professor Luther agreed, "I imagine so. However, if something is wrong with your church, you can't just stomp off and start your own. It makes much more sense to try and make it better from the inside out. I love God, I love our church, and I would like it to reform and bring its behavior into line with what God's Word says in His Scriptures."

Max shuddered. "Professor Luther, it's probably dangerous even to talk to you anymore."

Professor Luther nodded. "It probably is, Max, so if you don't want to, I really understand."

Max shook his head. "No matter what the Holy Father says," he said slowly, "I will stick with you as long as you'll let me, and I intend to be supportive of you. But please be careful, Professor."

Max was right. The pope was very angry.

Tetzel's indulgences were featured in Luther's list of 95. Tetzel howled and raged against Luther, shouting, "I have orders from His Holiness himself to burn at the stake anyone who opposes the sale of indulgences. Anyone who does not buy these indulgences is refusing God's forgiveness."

Professor Luther stood calmly and responded with Scripture to everything he was accused of. This seemed to frustrate his accusers more and more. Word was soon passed back to Rome.

Pope Leo X roared in anger and immediately began drafting a set of papers called "The Bull of Excommunication." In this bull, or document, the pope ordered Luther to appear in Worms in April 1521 to recant or else be burned at the stake.

In the meantime Frederick the Wise, the ruler of Saxony and founder of the university, would protect Luther.

WITTENBERG, GERMANY: DECEMBER 10, 1520

"Professor Luther! Professor Luther!" Max called.

"Yes, Minim," he answered. Maximilian had grown taller now. He had been a student of Professor Luther's for three years and was no longer a short, skinny little boy. But Professor Luther still called him Minim, as if he were.

"There's a message for you here from the pope!"

"Oh, my," said Luther. "Sounds like there will be action here today."

"Oh, please be careful, Professor Luther," Max pleaded. "You know that he has demanded several times for you to be turned over to him. Frederick the Wise has protected you so far, but he can do only so much."

"He has protected me because that is God's plan," Professor Luther said, "and he listens to it. That's why we call him Frederick the Wise."

Max laughed. "How can you joke at a time like this? Come, we must find out what the message is."

"Probably just more of the pope's thunder," Luther muttered, but he quickened his steps to match Max's.

* * *

"Excommunicated? He has excommunicated me? He can't cut me off from the love of Christ!" Luther shouted. He gathered up the message and several other papers and started out the door. Friends and students followed him. By the time he reached the gates of Wittenberg, there was a large crowd.

"What is he going to do?" Frank, a friend of Max's, asked.

"I don't know," Max said. "But it's bound to be exciting."

Frank asked, "Why did the pope excommunicate him?"

"You have missed a lot of the excitement by not being in school here the past three years," Max said, feeling much older and wiser than his younger friend. "Professor Luther has been very famous for studying the Scriptures. He feels that our church puts too much emphasis on unimportant things and on some things that are just plain wrong and should never have had any emphasis. The four main things he preaches are: Christ alone, the Bible alone, faith alone, and grace alone. This is upsetting to anybody who likes a lot of power through the church."

"I guess it would be," Frank said. "Sort of cuts out the middle man, doesn't it? It makes religion a thing between a person and God instead of something that has to go through a priest or series of them."

"Yes," nodded Max, "but I believe he's right."

"So what's he going to do?" Frank asked.

Max laughed a nervous sort of laugh. "Knowing Professor Luther, I have no clue," he said. "Anything is possible."

Outside the gates, Luther threw together some sticks. He purposefully wadded up the papers, including the message from the pope, and set them on fire. The crowd caught its breath in horror.

"What is he doing?" asked Frank again.

"Shh," whispered Max, "I'll explain later."

"But why did he set that on fire?" asked Frank. "Setting someone's writing on fire is calling them a heretic. Is Professor Luther calling the pope a heretic?"

"Shh!" Max frowned, and nodded.

Frank laughed. "Wow! So Professor Luther is excommunicating the pope back, isn't he?"

"Shh," cautioned Max, and nodded again.

Max was worried for his friend. He had no idea how far-reaching this day's actions would be. But I had an idea, and I was grateful for the host of guardians gathered around Wittenberg at the bonfire that day. Professor Luther and his friends would need them.

CITY OF WORMS, GERMANY: A.D. 1521

Max looked into the eyes of his friend and sat down across from him.

"So what happened?" Frank asked.

"I knew that our elector of Saxony," Max started, "no matter how important he was—even if he did found the University of Wittenberg—would not be able to protect the professor forever."

"Yeah, you've said that before," Frank said, "but what happened today?"

"A lot of the same stuff that has been going on," answered Max. "The emperor was there, and all the dignitaries of the empire, and many representatives from Rome. They kept questioning Professor Luther about all the things he had said. Professor

Luther kept telling them the same things over and over:

"He believes in Christ alone.

"He doesn't believe that Christ needs any help to save us—that what He did was enough.

"He believes in the Bible alone. He doesn't believe that the church should add and take away anything—that we should just accept the Scriptures the way they were written.

"He believes that God's people should live by faith alone and not have to try continually to earn their way to heaven. And he believes that we are saved by His grace alone."

"Yes, yes," Frank said. "He has told us those things many times. But what was the bottom line, because it's over, isn't it?"

Max nodded. "Yes, they asked him if he would recant his writings."

"Recant?"

"Yes," Max said, "you know, admit he was wrong—take it back."

Frank nodded. "Oh, yes. But what did Professor Luther say?"

"I was proud of him," answered Max. "I can remember almost exactly the way he said it."

Max stood tall and mimicked Professor Luther's accent. "I cannot submit my faith either to the pope or to the councils, because it is clear as day they have frequently erred and contradicted each other. Unless therefore I am convinced by the testimony of Scripture . . . I cannot and will not retract. Here I stand. I can do no other. So help me God. Amen."

Frank drew a deep breath. "Are they going to execute him?" he asked.

"They didn't say that officially," Max said, "but I'm very worried about him. During this whole trial here Spanish soldiers from Emperor Charles have been ransacking the town, trying to find and burn all the copies of Professor Luther's book."

"*The Babylonian Captivity of the Church?*" Frank asked.

"Yes, that one. As angry as everyone is, I'm afraid they'll do something bad to him whether or not it is the decision of the council."

"Well," Frank said, "my uncle is worried about that too, and he has a plan."

Max glanced around him, making sure no one could overhear them. "What is it?" he asked.

"My uncle lives in Wartburg Castle."

"Oh, yes," Max said. "I know of him."

"Well, he wanted Professor Luther to come there and hide for safety, but of course Professor Luther wouldn't do that, so my uncle has another plan. He wants several of us to kidnap Professor Luther and carry him off to the castle. No one will know whether he was kidnapped by his enemies or his supporters, and we will hide him until the fury from this has died down and it will be safe for him to come out again. Can I count on you to help?"

Max's eyes shone with excitement. "Count me in," he said.

WARTBURG CASTLE: A.D. 1522

"Max!"

"Frank!"

The boys rushed over and hugged each other in the kitchen of the great castle.

"It's so good to see you again, Frank!"

"You too," Frank said. "What's been happening here?"

"Well," Max answered, "Professor Luther has been really depressed. He hasn't been happy about being kidnapped and being in hiding, even if it was by his friends."

"That's what I hear," Frank said, "but at least he was safe."

"Yes," Max added. "He grew a beard, and he looks like a

wild man now. He looks quite different than the professor we had in school."

"This I've got to see," Frank observed.

"I'm afraid not," Max said. "He's shaving it off this morning."

"He is?"

"Yes, in honor of going back to Wittenberg."

"Yeah, I heard that," Frank said. "That's why I'm back here. I've come to make the trip with you too, and my uncle.

"Are you sure this is a good idea? At least he was safe here in the castle. If he goes back to Wittenberg, everybody's going to know where he is. His enemies could kill him if they want to."

"I know," said Max, nodding. "But he's so unhappy here."

"I suppose," Frank mused. "Just sitting around a dingy old castle would make me depressed too."

"He hasn't been just sitting around," Max said. "He has been working on translating the Bible into German. He's part way through the New Testament."

"Into German?" Frank asked. "You mean so that people like us could just read it without learning our Latin?"

"Frank!" Max scolded. "You've been in school how long now? You should be able to read it in Latin. But yes, so that normal people could read it in German."

Frank laughed. "I'm no good at Latin," he said. "They've kept me in the school there only because my uncle is rich."

Max laughed. "Then maybe Professor Luther was translating it for you too. Anyway, he has stayed busy working on that, but he says that Satan has been harassing him and that the demons bother him so he can't sleep. One day he became so angry he turned around and threw his ink pot at the wall. It smashed and made a big splotch. He said he threw it at the devil, and he wouldn't let the maids wash it off the wall. He said it needed to stay there to remind the devil what was coming if he kept bothering him."

Frank chuckled. "Sounds like Professor Luther to me."

Max nodded. "He loves God and he works very hard, but he has quite a temper, doesn't he?"

Frank laughed. "It's a good thing that God uses people with character problems to do His work, or none of us would be able to do anything."

Max nodded. "That's right. There just aren't any perfect people around for God to use these days."

Frank laughed. "Was there ever?"

"So what's been happening on the outside?" Max asked. "I spend most of my time with Professor Luther doing chores and running up and down the stairs bringing things from the kitchen, and I don't hear much news from out there. Do people still remember Professor Luther?"

"Oh, yes," Frank replied. "There has been much fighting between Professor Luther's followers and those who still follow the church leaders. Lots of people have died."

"That's terrible."

"Oh, it's worse than that," Frank continued. "Professor Luther has been misrepresented. Many of his followers are sensible people, but all of the nuts who were unhappy with church leadership before have jumped on his bandwagon and claimed to be followers of Luther, but they're just as crazy as they were before, and they give him a really bad reputation."

"What do you mean?" asked Max.

"Well, there's this guy named Jan Bockelson."

"That strange man from Münster?"

"He claims to be a follower of Luther. However, he says that he is the reincarnation of King David, and that the Second

Coming will be soon. He has taken as many wives as possible to make lots of children before Jesus comes again."

"More than one wife?" Max asked incredulously.

"Yes," Frank said. "He had 15 before the government came and sieged the town. Eventually they starved the people into submission. They opened it up and turned Bockelson over to them."

"What happened to him?" Max asked.

"Oh, they killed him," Frank explained. "There's been a lot of that out there. Mr. Bockelson isn't the only weird person who gives Professor Luther a bad reputation."

"H'mmm." Max was thoughtful. "That's one reason Professor Luther wants to come back out and lead his people. It seems that if there is so much fighting and so much confusion that they do need leadership."

"Yes," Frank said. "And I suppose that if God wants him to lead His people, He is able to protect him too."

Max nodded. "And us, since we hang around with him."

Frank's eyes shone. "I wouldn't miss this for anything."

"Me neither," Max answered. "Let's go upstairs and see if he is ready to go."

EPILOGUE

The Most High did protect Professor Luther as well as Max and Frank and many of His other followers, although some of the others did pay for their commitment with their blood. Three years after Professor Luther returned to Wittenberg, he married—being no longer a priest of the Catholic Church. By this time both Max and Frank had completed their studies at Wittenberg and returned to their homes— Frank to his wealthy relatives, Max to his family. Both of them continued to share what they had learned and to spread the beginnings of the Reformation through Germany.

As I watched them and recorded the events in the heavenly

archives two things stood out in my mind. As long as there has been organized religion, there have always been people who tried to use it to control others. Why humans have this need for control has never been clear to me. Perhaps it is just part of the sinful condition that humans suffer from. Control has never been part of the Most High's plans. He even was willing to give His Son to die to restore freedom of choice to humans, and the very ones who spread the good news of salvation were often the ones who turned around and tried to control others through religion. The Most High desires humans to worship Him and love Him with all their hearts. It has always seemed to me that humans would be better off concentrating on that instead.

The other thing that seems to occur again and again is that humans seem very uncomfortable just accepting God's gift. Trying to earn it themselves somehow is at the base of every false religion I have observed and recorded for the archives from the earliest times. Even among the followers of Christ who were given the free gift of salvation, there seems to be a need to somehow earn it by their behavior. Do humans not understand that this is impossible? If they could see what I see, they would just throw themselves at the feet of the Most High and say, "Oh, thank You! Thank You!"

I guess humans can't see what I see. And those of us who work as guardians and recorders have to be patient. Perhaps someday we will understand the soft spot the Most High has for these frail creatures. For now, we do our jobs as we've been instructed: caring for them, protecting them, and continuing to watch.

GEOFFREY

eoffrey hung onto the rail as he walked along the slippery deck. Even through the thick fog, he knew his way to the captain's quarters, for he had grown up there. When Mama died, Papa could have left him with relatives, but he didn't. As captain of his own ship, Papa had brought him along. Geoffrey felt very grown up now that he was 8 years old and able to do many tasks on the ship. However, he was the only crew member who got to sleep in the captain's quarters and to eat at the table with Papa.

"Geoffrey," Papa said, "please go down to the passenger cabin and check on Father Knox. Empty his chamber pot if he needs it."

Geoffrey wrinkled his nose. "Ew! He doesn't do that himself?"

It wasn't that Geoffrey didn't want to do what Papa had asked him. It was just unusual. However, between the fog and the rain, this voyage had been much longer and rougher than most of their crossings. The few passengers they took on their boat usually brought their own servants to take care of such things.

"No," Papa explained, "he has no servants. I believe this is a secret crossing. He doesn't seem to want to be seen out on deck, unless, of course, he's just seasick."

Geoffrey and Papa both laughed. A lot of big tough guys from land turned into whimpering babies when they got out on a sea crossing like this. Geoffrey stood a little taller. He never got seasick.

"OK," he said, "I'll go check on him."

Geoffrey knocked on the door of the passenger cabin and then entered. It was dark, so he struck the flint and lit a candle, setting it on the shelf next to the hammock hanging in the corner. A tall man lay in the hammock looking miserable. By his black robes and white collar, Geoffrey guessed he must be a priest, and by the smell of the room, he seemed a very seasick priest.

"Papa sent me to check on you," he said.

"Oh," the priest groaned. "Tell him thank you."

"Here, let me take that," Geoffrey said. "If I empty it, the room won't smell so bad, and maybe you'll feel better. I can get you a drink of water too." As he returned, the priest seemed a little more awake.

"Thank you, son," he said. "What's your name?"

"I am Geoffrey," he said. "My father is the captain of this ship."

"Ah, it seems that you are a much better sailor than I am."

Geoffrey laughed. "I learned to walk on this ship. I've been at sea all my life, even if it is just the English Channel."

"Apparently, it can get as rough out here as it does anywhere else," the priest observed.

Geoffrey laughed. "Yes, you look like you've been on some pretty rough seas this afternoon."

The priest smiled in spite of his obvious discomfort. "If we don't get into port soon," Geoffrey offered, "I'll come back and check on you in a little while."

"That would be fine," the priest said. "I could use the distraction."

"You could come up on deck," Geoffrey suggested. "Perhaps the fresh air would do you good."

All of a sudden the priest seemed less friendly and more withdrawn. "It's best I stay in my cabin," he said.

"Whatever you like," Geoffrey replied. "I'll see you later." He headed back to report to his papa.

"Well, we were both right," Geoffrey said, bursting into his papa's cabin. "He is seasick, and he also seems to want to stay hiding in his room for some reason. Do you think he's a criminal?"

Papa laughed. "I don't think so," he said, "although it's possible. He could be a heretic. There has been quite a traffic of heretics back and forth to Scotland lately."

"Why?" Geoffrey asked.

"There's a war on in Scotland right now," Papa said. "It's been going about two years. The Scottish nobles are heretics, but the queen is still a good Catholic."

"But I thought the Queen of Scotland was in France," interrupted Geoffrey.

"Yes, she is the queen of France too, so she lives there with her husband. Her mother, Mary of Guise, runs Scotland for her. She has done that since Mary was a baby, because she became the Queen of Scotland when she was only 6 days old! The English king was hoping to betroth her to little Prince Edward when they were still little children. Mary of Guise infuriated them by smuggling the tiny queen across the Channel and betrothing her to the Dauphin of France instead. Anyway, the heretics are trying to force her to convert and change the government of Scotland to a Protestant government instead."

"Protestant?" Geoffrey asked.

"Yes, that's a word that the heretics use sometimes. It comes from the word 'protest,' which is what they've been doing against the Catholic Church."

"Ah," Geoffrey said, "so 'Protestant' means people who protest."

"Yes, they like that better than heretic, but we believe they're heretics. They should all be burned at the stake."

"Ew!" Geoffrey exclaimed. "Sounds awful!"

"Yes," Papa agreed, "it would be awful, but that's what we do with heretics."

Geoffrey went back out onto the deck to think about this. Hours later the fog had not lifted, and the little ship was still on the Channel. The guardians hovered over it. There was no chance of this ship sinking, for one of God's important people was on board, although he didn't look as thunderous and imposing with his head in a bucket from being seasick as he did thundering from the pulpit. Geoffrey slipped back into the passenger cabin to check on him again.

"I just came by to see how you were doing," Geoffrey said. As the priest looked up from the bucket he added, "Well, I guess I see how you're doing."

They both laughed. "Here," Geoffrey offered, "let me give you another drink of water. It isn't always this bad, you know."

The priest nodded.

"Well, I guess I can tell Papa that you're just seasick," Geoffrey announced. "He and I were talking, and we figured you were either seasick or a heretic hiding so that no one would recognize you."

The man raised an eyebrow and looked at Geoffrey.

"I'm really glad you're not a heretic. Papa says they burn them."

The man was quiet for a minute and said, "Some people might call me that."

"Really?" said Geoffrey. "Are you a real heretic? Wow! On our ship and everything?"

The man smiled. If he hadn't been so nauseated, he might have even laughed.

"Are you a famous heretic?" Geoffrey asked. "Or just an unimportant one?"

"We're all important to God," the man replied.

"Ah, yeah, I know," Geoffrey said. "I mean to the rest of us."

The man smiled at Geoffrey. "Right this minute you might be even more important to God than I am."

Geoffrey paused to think for a moment.

I smiled. How could any human's value to God be measured? The Almighty had already said that He would provide the life of His Son in exchange for any one of them, so all were of such tremendous value that it would boggle their human minds if they had any idea. However, right now the Almighty was using young Geoffrey, even though he was only 8 years old, to help care for His servant crossing the Channel to Scotland.

"You know," the priest continued, his voice getting a little stronger, "God has a particular soft spot in His heart for young lads. He's used them many times in His work."

"Really?" Geoffrey asked. "Like who?"

"Well, in the Bible there's a story of a young lad who brought his lunch, and Jesus used it and multiplied it until it was able to feed five thousand people."

"That's awesome," Geoffrey breathed. "I wish Jesus could use *me* for something."

"He can," the priest replied. "Not many years ago He used a young lad not much older than you."

"He did? What was his name?" Geoffrey asked

"His name was Edward," the priest said. "He was a special friend of mine."

"Tell me about him," Geoffrey demanded.

"Edward was a young prince," the priest continued. "His father died when he was still a lad. He was determined to help his people get to know God better and to understand what God wanted from them—without all of the confusion that the church has brought in."

"Oh, Edward was a heretic?"

"Well, that's not what we called him," the priest answered. "We called him, 'Your Majesty.'"

"Oh, you're talking about young King Edward."

"Yes," he said. "I was his royal chaplain. Edward wanted very much to help England be a good Protestant country. I was working on *The Book of Common Prayer* that we were preparing during his reign."

"But Edward is dead," observed Geoffrey.

"Yes," the priest answered. "That was very sad, and his sister was very determined for England to be a good Catholic country. I had to run for my life to Europe. Many other people have lost their lives and have been burned at the stake."

"Are you the great heretic Knox?" Geoffrey asked.

The priest looked at the floor, then nodded.

"I've heard of you," Geoffrey said. "They've been watching for you a long time."

"I imagine they have," Mr. Knox replied. "I didn't tell you this so that you could make a lot of money collecting a bounty from the English soldiers. I told you this because I want you to know how important you are to God. He loves you and has a job for you to do too."

"He does? But I'm not a prince or anyone important."

"Well, neither am I," Mr. Knox replied, "but the Lord has a job for all of us."

Geoffrey paused to consider this. "Has your job been to hide the past few years in Europe?"

"Oh no. I was hiding from the English soldiers, but I went to Geneva and I learned a lot from another famous preacher."

"Is he another heretic?" Geoffrey asked, his eyes sparkling.

"Yes," replied Mr. Knox. "His name is Calvin. He lives in Geneva."

"Oh, I've heard of him. He's another heretic that the church would like to get its hands on. His first name is John."

"Yes," Mr. Knox said, "so is mine."

Geoffrey was delighted. For the next hour Mr. Knox continued to tell him all about the things he had learned from Mr. Calvin in Switzerland. It seemed that no time had passed at all before Geoffrey heard his father calling him.

"Geoffrey, where are you? Get yourself up here on deck. We're nearing port."

"I've got to go," Geoffrey said.

Mr. Knox put his hand on Geoffrey's head. "God will bless you, Geoffrey," he said. "Don't forget your job."

Geoffrey nodded and ran up on deck. As he helped his father with the preparations for docking in the English harbor of Hull, he kept asking himself: *What job does God want me to do? Does God want me to tell the soldiers where the famous heretic is hiding?* Geoffrey shuddered. He couldn't imagine the thin man who had been so seasick being dragged away by soldiers. Even worse was the idea of him chained to a stake in flames. No, surely God had something else in mind.

As the sailors carried the freight from France off the ship the tall stranger in his black cloak slipped down the gangplank and into the crowd. He had no luggage. And in a moment he blended in and was gone. Geoffrey watched him go. He was glad he hadn't told. But he wondered if it was a sin not to tell on heretics and if God was mad at him.

I drew close. Geoffrey was the type of boy whom God could use. Mr. Knox was right. As long as his heart was open, I knew that the Almighty would send His Spirit to guide him and help him understand that sin is just separation from God—a very human condition—and that it is not necessary to tell on others so that they could be dragged away and burned to please the

84

Almighty. He had been very clear in His Word about how to please Him. Humans just needed to find out what that was. And I knew that even an illiterate boat boy like Geoffrey would learn.

ENGLISH CHANNEL: A.D. 1560

For days Geoffrey continued to think about the heretic Mr. Knox and all of the things he had told him. So many of the things Mr. Knox had said made good logical sense, but Geoffrey was confused. He and Papa had always been Catholic, and although they weren't in port very often, Geoffrey had gone to church when they were and made his confession to the priest. Business was good in the following weeks, and Geoffrey and his father had had no opportunities to see a priest in port, for their ship was busy going back and forth across the Channel.

Geoffrey felt as if he would burst if he couldn't talk to someone or get some answers. Finally one day in his cabin he remembered something Mr. Knox had said—that humans didn't really need a middleman. Would God be willing to listen directly to them without going through the proper channels, like a priest? What if Mr. Knox was wrong? What if he tried to talk to God and it made God angry? Geoffrey had an anxious little ball of fear growing in his stomach, but he felt if he couldn't get some answers soon, he would just burst.

Kneeling in his father's cabin, he said, "God, I know that You're King of the universe and that You're very important, and I know that I'm only a cabin boy on a Channel ship and I'm not very important, but I just have to talk to You. I haven't been able to see a priest for a long time. I hope You don't mind—Mr. Knox said You wouldn't. I hope Mr. Knox is a friend of Yours." Geoffrey paused. Suddenly a great feeling of peace filled him.

I backed up to my perimeter of the room out of respect. The Spirit of the Almighty was present. It was as amazing to me as it would have been to Geoffrey could he have seen who was there. The Spirit, ruler of the universe, chose to be in that tiny ship cabin at the beckoning of a young boy. The passion with which the Almighty loves these humans is overwhelming even to those of us who have seen it again and again. There in the cabin He gently nudged Geoffrey's memory and helped him remember things he had been taught. Having only human sight, Geoffrey may not have been able to see Him, but it was obvious he could feel His presence, and he continued to pray.

ENGLISH CHANNEL: A.D. 1561

"Papa," Geoffrey asked, "what was the royal messenger visiting you about?" Geoffrey had been dying to ask ever since they had left the English harbor.

Papa smiled grimly. "He brought some news and a warning from the queen," he said. "You know that the king of France died last week."

"Yes," Geoffrey said. "That was sad. He was so young, almost the same age as me."

Father nodded. "He was almost twice your age, but still way too young to die," he said. "The young queen has been left a widow. She is still a teenager."

"That's very sad," Geoffrey said sadly. "However, she's still queen of France and of Scotland, isn't she?"

"Yes and no," Papa replied. "She is still the queen of Scotland, but in France, now that her husband has died, his younger brother has become king. He's not married yet, but his mother, Catherine of Médici, also a queen, is his adviser. She has never liked young Queen Mary, and I expect things are very uncomfortable for her there in the French court now."

Geoffrey nodded and then asked, "But Papa, why would the English queen send that type of news to us. Does she care?"

"Oh yes," Papa answered. "The English queen is a cousin of Mary, the young French queen, but they hate each other."

"Why?"

"Oh, many reasons," Papa said. "For one thing, the English queen is a Protestant, so Queen Mary of France and Scotland considers her a heretic. Also, remember that when Queen Mary was a baby, she had been promised to Elizabeth's brother, Edward. However, Queen Mary's family were Catholic, Edward was a Protestant, so the tiny queen was smuggled out of Scotland and taken to France, where she married the dauphin instead. When the dauphin's father died, he became king of France."

"Ah," Geoffrey said, "I can see why they wouldn't like each other."

"Oh, it's worse than that. Queen Elizabeth's mother married King Henry VIII only after he divorced his first wife. Since Catholics don't believe in divorce, they do not believe that Queen Elizabeth was a legitimate child, and therefore Queen Mary of France and Scotland would be the next closest relative."

"Ah," said Geoffrey, "so Catholics feel that Queen Mary, not Queen Elizabeth, should be the queen of England."

"That's right," Papa said. "The last queen of England, Queen Mary, was a Catholic. When Queen Elizabeth came to the throne, she chose not to continue making Britain be a Catholic country. So many of the loyal Catholics in England feel that Mary of France and Scotland should be queen of England too. Queen Elizabeth sent messages to all of the captains of ships back in English harbors asking us to watch for Mary. She's afraid Mary will try to come back across the Channel and may try to take the throne of England from her."

"Do you think she will?" Geoffrey asked.

"Well, apparently the thought has crossed her mind," said Papa, "since she calls herself the Queen of England as well. She

87

does not recognize Elizabeth's claim to the throne and includes that in her titles."

"Um," Geoffrey mused, "this could be interesting."

"Yes," his father agreed. "Our job is to run this boat back and forth in the Channel and take people where they need to go. I don't care what their religion or whom they serve as long as they pay for their passage."

Geoffrey smiled. He was glad his father felt that way. He knew that many of the people they had been transporting had been heretics. They had been leaving France in small groups, like Mr. Knox, some going to Scotland, some going to England. Others they took up the Channel, depositing them in Belgium and Holland. France was becoming a more difficult place for heretics to live every day.

Geoffrey enjoyed this. He'd had more opportunities to ask questions and had been receiving answers. He knew that transporting heretics was illegal in France and Scotland, so transporting the Queen of Scotland would make them lawbreakers in England too.

"We just don't ask questions," his papa advised. "The less we know, the better off we are, and if we don't know, we can't tell anyone, can we, now?"

Geoffrey smiled. He knew how to keep a secret.

CALAIS, FRANCE: AUGUST 19, 1561

"Wake up, Geoffrey!"

Geoffrey opened his eyes to see his father gently shaking his shoulder. "We have passengers. I need you to escort them to the cabin. Help them with their baggage and bolt the door. Once you have bolted the door from the inside, I will pile barrels and freight outside the door. I want you to stay with them during the crossing to reassure them."

Geoffrey nodded and sat up. This would not be the first time they had taken secret passengers who had boarded during the night. However, whoever it was must have paid extra and needed extra secrecy to have them covering up the door of the cabin. He threw on his clothes quickly and ran out onto the deck.

A small knot of people were hurrying up the plank.

"This way," he said as he led them into the cabin. There were three women in black and some men. One of the women was seated in the cabin, the other two huddled close to her. Geoffrey could not see their faces by the flickering lamplight, for they were wearing heavy black veils. Two of the men remained in the tiny cabin with the women; the rest bowed and kissed the hand of the seated woman and disappeared back out onto the deck.

"I have water and some bread and a little cheese here on the table," Geoffrey said. "If you have need of anything, please tell me."

One of the women turned to Geoffrey. "We need nothing," she said. "We have a few provisions with us too. All we need is a safe crossing."

Geoffrey nodded. He closed the door and brought the large bar down into the latch.

He could hear his father stacking crates against the door on the outside. Geoffrey leaned against the barred door. *This is going to be a long voyage,* he thought. He wished he could be out on the deck helping his father instead of being cooped up in the tiny room.

Geoffrey was right—it was a long voyage. His mind wandered as he stood guarding the door. Could this be the queen they had been warned of seeking passage to Scotland on their little boat? It seemed unlikely, yet surely if she was trying to cross the Channel without being detected by the English ships, a tiny boat like theirs would be more likely to make it.

Since his talk with Mr. Knox, Geoffrey had been thinking

through many of the things he had always believed in. *I guess I'm not really a good Catholic anymore,* he thought. *Many of the things Mr. Knox said made much sense to me.* Yet his brow wrinkled as he thought, *I've talked to many heretics now, and it seems that each one believes something just a little different from the others. How do I know what's really true? I guess if I had been educated as a priest, perhaps I could read the Scriptures for myself. A few Scriptures are available out there, but they are so expensive and hard to find—and illegal in most places.*

He frowned. It was true what Mr. Knox had said about many of the church leaders being corrupt, and yet he thought about recent years in England. King Henry VIII had become a Protestant, and he did not seem to be much of a saint. He had problems with adultery and cut off the heads of people who didn't agree with him. It was confusing.

Perhaps, Geoffrey thought to himself, *perhaps I'm not a Catholic or a Protestant or a follower of any one of these people. Perhaps I'm just a follower of Jesus, and if I continue to pray and ask, He'll help me learn what is right and what He wants me to do.*

His gaze shifted to the woman in black seated across from him. As a follower of Jesus, should he assist the Catholic queen? Would it be wrong to help her escape to Scotland to lead her people there against the Protestants? Or would it be wrong to betray her and let someone know who she was and where she was, knowing that that would lead to her death?

Geoffrey sighed. Surely it must have been easier for Christians during other times in history. These times just seemed so hard. How could he know what God wanted him to do? He closed his eyes, asking for help.

I drew close to him. His guardians were close too—as well as several others hovering over the tiny craft. With a sigh Geoffrey opened his eyes again. It was impossible for a 10-year-old to figure out all the answers, but surely as a follower of Jesus he should be kind to all of the passengers on his boat, whether they were Catholic queens or heretics. He shifted his weight to the other foot. Yes, that was answer enough for him right now.

As they pulled in to port, he could hear the hands up on deck running back and forth, working the sails and hauling ropes. The loud scraping of boxes being moved let him know it was almost time to get off. As the last box was moved, he lifted the heavy bar and opened the door.

Papa was on the other side, and when the door opened he bowed deeply. "Your Majesty," he said. The lady in black stood and walked over to him. She lifted the black veil from her face and looked at him, her eyes peering deep into his.

Geoffrey noticed big dark circles under her eyes. She looked as if she had done a lot of crying.

"Thank you for your kindness," she said.

Papa spoke. "Your Majesty, we are at the Scottish port of Leith. You have arrived safely."

She looked at Geoffrey. "Legends say that those who drink from the river of Leith forget everything they've seen."

Geoffrey nodded.

"We will all drink its water this morning," Geoffrey's father assured her.

She nodded and lowered the veil back over her face, then stepped out onto the deck. As Geoffrey followed her out, he noticed a large group of soldiers waiting at the bottom of the gangplank. With a sigh of relief he noticed the Scottish royal family's coat-of-arms on their banner. They had delivered the queen safely.

ENGLISH CHANNEL: AUGUST 25, 1572

Geoffrey stared down the gangplank and into the seaside port of Calais. He made his way to his usual inn and sat down at one of the tables. "Monsieur Geoffrey, it's good to see you again," said the innkeeper. "Dinner?"

"Yes," Geoffrey said.

"A bowl of stew for Mr. Geoffrey," the innkeeper shouted to the young lady running back and forth to the kitchens. "And bring him something to drink."

"Yes, Papa," she replied.

The innkeeper sat down across from Geoffrey. "How's business?" he asked.

"Good," Geoffrey said. "We've been staying busy and have had full cargo both ways."

"H'mm," grunted the innkeeper. "Are you booked for the passage back?"

"Not yet," Geoffrey said. "You have contacts for me?"

"H'mm," the innkeeper muttered, "but they are very fond of secrets. They wish their cargo to be handled carefully, and the men shipping it wish to travel in the cargo hold with their cargo."

Geoffrey nodded. "It could be done, I suppose," he said. "When can I meet them?"

"When they bring their cargo. If you're back to your ship by 10:00 tonight, they will be ready to board."

Geoffrey nodded. It was not uncommon for people to want to load their cargo at night or to guard it if they were shipping valuables. Geoffrey was 21 years old now, and his father had put him in charge of all the cargo shipping. His father ran the ship and the crew. Business was good, and Geoffrey and his father were planning to buy a second ship by the time Geoffrey was 26. Then each would be a captain.

At 10:00 Geoffrey was back on his ship. He had opened the hold and was ready to receive cargo right on time. Four men emerged from the shadows, carrying two very large wicker trunks.

"Here, my crew will help you," Geoffrey offered.

"No," they said. "Thank you, but our belongings are very fragile and very valuable, and we must carry them ourselves."

Geoffrey shrugged. "As you wish."

The men returned to land, and soon brought two more of the large basket trunks up the gangplank.

"How many of those do you have?" Geoffrey inquired.

"Twelve," they answered.

"We have room for more cargo than this," Geoffrey grumbled. "I thought you said this was a full load."

"We'll pay for the full cargo," one of the men volunteered.

Geoffrey nodded. He thought he heard the sound of coughing coming from the cargo hold, but then two of his crew and one of the men in black started coughing violently too. It was hard to tell. The men quickly carried their heavy baskets up onto the ship.

"We will sail immediately?" they asked.

"As you wish," Geoffrey said. "We've restocked all of our provisions this evening, and our crew is on board."

The man nodded. "We'll sit in the cargo hold with our belongings." Geoffrey nodded. The men lowered themselves into the hold, and he closed the trapdoor from the deck.

Why anyone would want to ride down there in the musty darkness was beyond him. It wasn't, however, beyond me. I watched the clusters of guardians steadying each basket with its precious cargo as the men carried it up the gangplank. Still others stood along the docks holding back the forces of darkness and closing the eyes of anyone who might notice anything odd.

Shortly after they left the port of Calais, Geoffrey, standing on the deck, heard a cry. He listened for some time and then heard it again, but it was quickly muffled.

I watched as a look of understanding swept across his face. He went to the cabin and lit a lantern, then he opened the trap door and slowly climbed down the ladder. He heard a frantic shuffling as he climbed down in silence.

The four men stood.

"It's OK," Geoffrey whispered. "You are safe. No one will hurt you here. I am one of you."

The men said nothing and looked at the floor, but a curly little head popped up from behind one of the baskets.

"Did you hear that?" he said. "He's one of us!"

Color drained from the men's faces. "Get down," one hissed.

Geoffrey laughed. "It's OK. Why don't you let them all out of their basket prisons until we get into harbor? No one will disturb you down here. I will be back in a few minutes."

"Don't go," said the little voice.

Geoffrey smiled. "Shall I leave the lantern here?"

One of the men nodded. "Thank you, Monsieur. He's afraid of the dark."

"But I try not to be," the little voice added. "Papa told me the angel of the Lord camps round about little boys and takes care of them."

"That's right," Geoffrey said, "and maybe he even understands about being scared of the dark and sent me down here with a lantern for you."

The little boy smiled. "Do you think he understands about being hungry, too?" he asked.

"Yes, I think he does," Geoffrey agreed. "I'll be right back."

Geoffrey did return soon with a large loaf of French bread under his arm and a bag with cheese and grapes in it.

"Here you go," he said. "We don't keep much food on board because we do only Channel runs, and they're fairly short, but this should hold you over."

"Oh, thank you, Monsieur," the little boy responded. He fell upon the bread and cheese as if he hadn't eaten in weeks. By the time Geoffrey returned, several others were in the room, and the wicker trunks lay open. They were all sharing the bread and cheese and fruit snack that Geoffrey had brought.

"So tell me what has happened," Geoffrey invited. "I heard terrible things at the inn."

One of the men nodded. "It was terrible. I hear it was worse in Paris. The persecution had lightened up for some time. We thought everything was OK. Then suddenly, yesterday, all over France we were attacked. Word is that the Jesuit priest who's the spiritual adviser to the king told the people that by killing all the Protestants in France, they would be forgiven for their many sins."

"They must have committed an awful lot of sins," observed the little boy between mouthfuls of bread.

"Aye," Geoffrey said. "Perhaps."

"They killed so many in Paris that it is said blood flowed down the streets like a river. We were not in the city, but we had to go around several villages to reach Calais. The rivers are so filled with bodies that the people may not eat fish for months because of the contamination. Already we saw wolves coming down from the hills to feed on the bodies lying in the roadways. It was terrible."

Geoffrey shuddered. "I know that many have been leaving France. I guess those who have survived this terrible massacre will be more anxious to go."

"You are very good to help us," one of the women said, "and we thank you."

Geoffrey stayed and talked with the fugitives. The tousled little redhead curled up in his lap when his tummy was full and fell asleep. Geoffrey heard more about the horrors of the massacre on St. Bartholomew's Day.

After a time he said, "I must get back up on deck."

He deposited the little boy in the arms of his daddy and

climbed back onto the deck. As he was just setting the trapdoor, he noticed one of the deckhands watching him. A small shaft of light was coming from the cargo hold.

Geoffrey jumped. "I, uh, I uh, left my lantern down in the hold," he said. "I will be going back down there in just a moment to retrieve it."

The deckhand nodded and then said softly, "The little one is my nephew." Geoffrey smiled. "I suppose that was you coughing to cover up for him?"

"Yes, sir."

"You're a good man," said Geoffrey. The deckhand disappeared into the shadows, and Geoffrey went to find his father.

ENGLISH CHANNEL: A.D. 1573

"So what is our cargo today?" asked Geoffrey's father. Then, glancing at his son, he said, "No, never mind. Don't tell me. It's best I don't know these things."

Geoffrey smiled. "Just valuable cargo, Papa," he said.

His father shook his head. "You are determined to take such risks."

"I have to," Geoffrey said. "They're killing people in France. We have to help them escape."

"I suppose," his father replied. "It's good for business."

"It does not seem to be good for France's business, though," Geoffrey pointed out.

"How so?" asked his father.

"Well, as I talk with the 'cargo,' all seem to be skilled workers. They are weavers and textile merchants, skilled jewelers, and silk weavers. It seems that France is losing her best manufacturing skills. Either they kill them or send them to be galley slaves in the French navy, or else we're helping them to escape to other countries."

His father nodded. "I hear the whole group of clockmakers is gone from Paris—either dead or escaped to Switzerland. And many of the skilled jewel-cutters have moved to Belgium."

"It's true," Geoffrey said. "And we've taken many of the weavers and textile experts to England and Holland."

"No, no, I didn't want to know that," Papa warned him.

"Right," Geoffrey answered.

"It doesn't seem right, though," Papa said. "I heard that when the news of last year's massacre reached the Vatican, instead of the pope's being upset with his people for such bloodshed, there was a great celebration. He had a commemorative medal struck to honor the occasion and even commissioned the artist, Vasari, to paint a mural of the massacre. Can you imagine?"

"No," Geoffrey answered, "I can't. He's no longer my spiritual leader. We can look only to Jesus as a good example, because our church leaders do not provide that."

"Son!" Papa warned. "Don't let anyone else hear you say that."

"Papa, had you noticed that he even uses a red dragon as his heraldic symbol on his coat of arms?"

"Yes. So?"

"But the Scriptures use that symbol for the devil."

"Geoffrey, let's not talk about this anymore," Papa said nervously.

"You know, Papa," Geoffrey predicted, "before this is over, I think all of us will have to choose whether we are going to do things the way God asked us to or the way people asked us to. In the end none of us will be able to look to any human leader. We will just have to find out what God really wants us to do and follow Him."

Papa nodded. "Maybe so," he said. "But I'm uncomfortable making a decision that carries such grave penalties."

Geoffrey laughed. "Yes, but you support me in my decision,

and you've protected all these shiploads of cargo all this time. I think I know where your heart really lies."

Papa looked at his feet.

"God knows too," Geoffrey said softly, "and He will help you keep understanding things until you make a decision. Meanwhile, I love you and I appreciate your loyalty."

"Well, uh, yeah," Papa mumbled gruffly. "I guess we better get to that cargo, huh?"

"I guess," Geoffrey agreed.

EPILOGUE

Geoffrey, through his example, influenced many people, and his father became a Protestant too. They were responsible for helping many Huguenots and Anabaptists escape from France and settle in other European countries.

Geoffrey was right—it was a great drain on some of France's most talented workers. France lost its best manufacturers and merchants, either to the sword, to the galleys, or to other countries.

By refusing to allow people to follow what the Scriptures said and trying to force them to follow church leaders and traditions, the country's greatest assets were drained. It would not be long before France would be bankrupt and brought to its knees, and a time of even greater bloodshed was looming on the horizon.

Still, those who escaped carried light to all the countries they went to, and God's Word continued to be spread throughout Europe. While many of the Most High's servants died during this time, the guardians were able to defend many as they escaped from France.

Monique

FRANCE, A.D. 1789-1794

PALACE OF VERSAILLES: JUNE 17, 1789

t was a perfect day. The sky was blue, and the sun was shining. The tinkling of the harpsichord mixed with strains of violin music. The luxury spread as far as Monique's eyes could see—it all made her feel as if she were in the most wonderful place on earth.

Surely it was. King Louis' palace at Versailles had to be the most luxurious palace in the world. There was gold everywhere, velvet and brocades, the most expensive hand-carved furniture covered in gold leaf, and the gardens and fountains outside. It took Monique's breath away and almost made up for having to stand around listening to boring grown-up talk.

Suddenly the captain of the guard hurried up to the king. "Your Majesty," he said in a low voice. "The peasants are revolting in Paris."

King Louis answered him loudly. "What's that? Speak up. You say the peasants are revolting? They certainly are, and they smell bad too."

Everyone roared with laughter. The captain bowed again.

"Your Majesty, they have nothing to eat. They are starving."

"Well, that's hardly something I can deal with this afternoon," the king said.

"But, Your Majesty, they have no bread."

"Then let them eat cake," a woman's voice called out from across the room.

Monique spun around to see who had spoken. The ladies were all grouped around the queen. Everyone was laughing and repeating, "Yes, let them eat cake." Monique shook her head. Grown-ups could be so silly.

"Come on, Prince Louis," she said to a boy beside her. "Let's go outside."

"You're supposed to call me 'Your Royal Highness,'" young Louis complained.

"All right, Your Royal Highness, let's go outside," she said.

"Sounds good to me," Louis said, and they slipped out through the double doors.

"Why do you think everyone in Paris is so hungry?" asked Monique.

"My tutor says that Paris used to be a place where many things were made and sold, and exported to other countries, but many of the people who worked there were heretics who had to be killed, or who escaped. This caused less money to come into France, and less taxes for Papa to run the government with."

Monique nodded. "That makes sense. So can't your papa send them some money to buy some bread?"

"It's not that easy," Louis said. "He needs the money he has for the palace and our parties and things like that."

"It doesn't seem right, if people are hungry," Monique observed. "So much of what's in there on that banquet table is going to waste. It makes me feel sad for the people who don't have any."

"Ugh! You talk like a republican, and anyway, girls aren't

supposed to worry about politics." He reached into the fountain and splashed water on her.

"No!" she squealed. "Nanette will have a fit if I get this dress wet. I already spilled something on the last one she put me in this afternoon."

Louis laughed. "I bet you can't catch me," he cried, and took off running for the stables.

Monique returned to her family's apartment in the palace, laughing and out of breath. She paused in the hallway as she heard angry voices.

"Who do they think they are?" her father shouted. "They can't control the king like this. They should all be executed."

"Perhaps they will be," her mother said.

Monique slipped in and hurried to her room.

"Where have you been?" cried Nanette. "Look at you! You're a mess!"

"Oh, Nanette, I've had a wonderful time!" Monique exclaimed.

Nanette arched an eyebrow. "Well, that's obvious. You look terrible. You've been out running around on the grounds again. Look! You've got mud all over your dress—I'm sure it's ruined."

Monique laughed. "Well, Louis has more mud on him than I do."

"Tsk, tsk, tsk!" Nanette clicked her tongue. "You can't call him Louis, even if he is your cousin. He is the dauphin, or His Royal Highness."

"OK," Monique said, "then the dauphin has more mud on him than I do."

"Well," Nanette sniffed, "he can do what he likes—he's the dauphin. You need to learn to act like a lady. You have the blood of kings in your veins—you must act like it."

"The dauphin has the blood of kings in his veins too," protested Monique as Nanette pulled her soiled dress off over her head.

"That's different," she snapped. "Anyway, today may not be a good day to be the king."

"What do you mean? Is that what Papa was shouting about?" Monique asked.

"I guess so," Nanette said. "I don't eavesdrop on your papa, but I heard him down in the kitchen saying that the king dissolved the Estates-General yesterday because it was not cooperating with him; today they met on a tennis court and formed their own government group called the National Assembly."

"Can they do that?" Monique asked.

"I don't know, but they did. Now we have to wait and see what the king does. I guess this is a power struggle between the people of Paris, who are angry at him because there is no food and because they're tired of fighting so many wars and being treated so badly, and the king, who feels he has every right to do that."

Monique shrugged. "Well, I'm sure the king will win, and they'll wish they hadn't done anything like that."

"H'mm, perhaps," Nanette mumbled.

"Have you heard any more about your little girl?" asked Monique.

"I got a letter this morning," said Nanette. "My mother says she is still very sick. I will be glad when your parents decide to go back to the chateau, and I can deal with her. I worry about her."

Monique nodded. "Since Mama and Papa are so upset about the National Assembly," she suggested, "perhaps this wouldn't be the best time to tell them that I ruined another dress while running through the orchard."

Nanette's eyes twinkled. "Just the orchard? Looks like you were dragging this skirt through the stables too."

"Well, there too," Monique confessed. "There is the most wonderful little foal out there. She was born just yesterday, and her legs are still a little bit wobbly."

Nanette laughed. "All right, you win. I won't tell this time, but you've got to start acting more like a lady."

I shook my head as I recorded the events of the day. Monique was going to have to grow up much faster than Nanette or anyone else had in mind.

AT THE FAMILY CHATEAU: AUGUST 4, 1789

The messenger rushed into the courtyard, his horse covered with sweat and flecked with foam. Anxious servants helped him off his horse. He stood shakily on his feet, obviously exhausted. "I must speak with the marquis immediately," he said. "I have a message for him from Paris."

A servant led him up to the marquis' study. Monique followed anxiously behind. What could be so important that a messenger would ride his horse half to death?

"My lord, marquis," he said, falling on one knee, "the National Assembly has abolished all feudal privileges."

"What?" the marquis shouted. "How dare they? Who do they think they are?"

Monique felt a hand on her shoulder. She spun around to see Nanette. "You are not to be in here eavesdropping on your father," she said, her face pale, but her jaw set and determined. "You must come with me now." Her grip on Monique's arm was firm as she dragged her down the stairs to the kitchen.

"What's the matter, Nanette? What are we doing? Why are you pulling me? Let go!" Monique protested, but Nanette just hurried faster. Arriving in the kitchen, she and the cook started pulling Monique's gold brocade gown off and ripping off the satin chemise beneath it.

"What are you doing? Stop!" she protested.

"Here, this will do," the cook said, pulling out a ragged, gray nondescript shift and dropping it over her shoulders. "Now wrap her in this cloak. There we go."

"You must come now," Nanette ordered. She pulled Monique out the door into the courtyard. There she picked up a small bundle of her belongings and, grabbing Monique firmly by the hand, headed down the road toward the entrance of the marquis' estate.

"Where are we going?" Monique asked. "Is this some kind of secret adventure?"

"Yes, sort of," Nanette said. "Let's hurry."

Monique was delighted. She had always wanted to go outside of the estate with Nanette, but had always been made to play within the estate grounds. Now she could see the world outside. She hurried along.

"Oh, stop," Nanette said. "This is silly." She looked down. Monique was garbed in her gray scratchy clothing with a very worn brown cloak and a hood with her green satin slippers poking out from under the dress.

"We'll have to wrap your feet," she said. "Many kids your age just have their feet wrapped anyway and don't have shoes, but we'll leave the shoes on underneath. It will make it easier for walking." She wrapped rags around Monique's feet. "There, that's better. Your feet almost gave you away."

Monique's eyes sparkled. Now no one would know who she really was.

"For today," Nanette instructed, "your name is Marie."

"The name of your daughter," Monique said.

Nanette's face clouded. "Yes, I miss her very much."

"I'm sad that she died," said Monique. "The consumption is terrible. It seems even when the best doctors are called, they cannot do much for it."

Nanette nodded and then said, "I have her papers here in my

bundle if we are stopped. You will answer to the name Marie while we are on our adventure."

"Yes, Maman," answered Monique. "I can call you Maman if my name is Marie, can't I?"

"Yes, that would be fine," laughed Nanette.

They soon reached the gates of the family estate. The guards did not even glance at Monique.

"Where are we going?" she asked.

"We're going south of here," Nanette replied. "We're going to go visit where I was born and where my family is."

"I thought your family lived here and worked for my papa," said Monique.

"Well, I lived here and worked for your papa, and my mother was a servant here, but I have aunts and cousins who live in the mountains to the south in the Vendée area. We are going there for a visit."

"Oh, what fun!" Monique exclaimed.

Nanette shot her a concerned glance. "It may not be fun," she said. "It could be a dangerous adventure. It's not safe for women to travel alone."

"But we'll be fine, won't we?"

"Yes," Nanette said firmly.

In the distance they saw a large group of people coming up the road. They seemed very angry and were armed with cudgels and pitchforks. "Death to the aristos! France for the citizens! France for the French! Down with the rich!" they shouted.

Nanette pulled Monique off to the side of the road. "Say nothing," she said, "no matter what they say to you."

The angry mob surged on past the two women. "Where are they going?" Monique asked. "Are they heading for the chateau? They are heading for the chateau. That's the only place this road goes."

"Yes," Nanette said. "You must stay with me."

"Are they going to talk to my papa?" she asked. "Surely he will tell them to go back to the village."

"We must hurry," Nanette said, as she kept pulling her farther and farther away from home.

"Nanette, I don't want to go. I want to find out what those angry people are going to do. Is my family safe? Surely the guards will not let them onto the estate."

As billows of smoke rose from the chateau they had left only an hour before, the guardians pressed close and covered the two frightened women with their wings.

"The smoke," Monique whispered. "It's the chateau."

"Yes," said Nanette.

"But what about Mama? What about Papa?" Monique whimpered in a quivering voice.

Nanette clasped her to her chest and rocked her back and forth. "I'm so sorry; I'm so sorry," she said. "I just couldn't bear to lose you. I lost my own Marie. I heard talk in the village last night of this. Monique, I've cared for you since you were a baby. I just couldn't bear to lose you too. Now I need to take you under my wing, and we need to do whatever it takes to survive. There are no more aristos in France. We will just be two women together. You must not speak to me as a servant anymore, but I will do everything in my power to protect you, and we will try to reach Vendée together where we might start a life again."

"But what about Mama? What about Papa?" Monique murmured again in shock.

"We will find a place on the other side of the next village. There are farms there, and we can sleep in a haystack where they are harvesting. Then we will check for news of the chateau. Don't worry, little one, I will keep you under my wing, and I will do everything I can to protect you."

I smiled. Nanette's wings might not be very strong, but

Monique was also under the wings of the guardians sent from the Almighty, and under His protection all the mobs in the world could not harm her.

The two women trudged forward in shocked silence, continuing to look over their shoulder at the blackening sky.

"No matter what has happened to your mama and papa," Nanette counseled, "always remember you have the blood of kings in your veins. Just be careful, and don't tell anyone when we are in enemy territory."

Monique walked a little taller.

I was thankful she could not see the terrible things happening at the chateau.

EN ROUTE TO VENDÉE (SOUTHERN FRANCE): OCTOBER 5, 1789

Monique and Nanette splashed in the chilly water. "Oh, Nanette, this feels good!" Monique cried. "I have never been this filthy. It's been a whole month since . . ." Her eyes clouded, then she raised her chin resolutely. ". . . since we started on this adventure. I was beginning to think I would never get to bathe again."

Nanette laughed. "I have been this filthy before, but it's been a long time. I miss life without warm water."

"Me too," Monique said, splashing, "but this just feels good, even if it is terribly cold." As they climbed back up the bank, Monique stood with her arms out waiting for Nanette to put the filthy gray shift back on her.

"Monique," hissed Nanette. "You must not do this. Peasant girls dress themselves."

"Oh, of course," Monique agreed, embarrassed. "I've just never done it. What do I do?"

"Start one piece at a time. Just do what I do," Nanette said. "Put on your undergarments, then pull the shift over your head. . . . Now wrap your beltpiece around your waist. Here, I'll tie it in the back for you. . . . Now your cloak. Very good. You'll soon get the hang of it."

Monique laughed. "It's a good thing I don't have to get dressed very often. It's dirty, and it smells bad to sleep in my clothes, but it does make life easy."

Nanette chuckled. "Well, don't get used to it. When we finally find my family and get moved in, you will have to bathe on a regular basis."

Monique laughed. "No problem." Then she added, "And another thing, when we have stopped in the villages, you have worked at farms and big houses for food, and you've always told them I was ill, and I sat in the barnyard and waited for you."

"Yes," said Nanette.

"I want to help you."

"What would you know how to do?" Nanette asked. "Aristo children don't know how to do anything."

"That's right," Monique said. "But I want you to teach me. If I'm going to be part of your family, then I need to know how to do something. I can't pretend to be ill all my life."

Nanette looked at her thoughtfully. She was developing more respect. The spoiled little aristo child had turned into a determined and brave young woman stubbornly trying to live the life she was given.

Monique looked at Nanette with new eyes too, having seen her work to provide food for the two of them. In each village they came to, she had always taken Nanette for granted. Now she realized Nanette was not only a wonderful chambermaid, but she could sew, do kitchen work, and milk cows and goats. Nanette knew how to churn butter and work the gardens. She knew which plants would have turnips on the other ends of them and which ones had to wait. How could she tell? They all looked green to Monique.

Their growing respect for each other made me smile as I recorded it. All of the friends of the Most High are given special gifts, and those who truly please Him will treat each other with respect. Monique and Nanette were learning. They just didn't know it.

It was approaching evening, and as they came upon the next village they stopped at the checkpoint to present their papers. Monique asked. "What news do you hear of Paris?"

"Ah," the soldier said, scanning their papers, "the National Assembly decided not to leave the king and that Austrian woman in their palace at Versailles, so they went and got them, and a mob moved them to Paris. You should have seen them, such cowards, shivering and shaking in their boots."

"Did they hurt them?" Nanette asked.

"No," the guard said. "They just put them in the palace of the Tuileries. It won't be as fancy as Versailles, but now that they are just citizens Louis and Marie Capet, they don't deserve even that."

Nanette nodded.

"They are rounding up as many aristos as possible," the soldier continued. "That's why we check everyone's papers—they're all trying to escape out of the country. I hear many of them are escaping to England."

"Really?" Monique asked, her eyes lighting up.

"Oui," the soldier affirmed. "But we're catching most of them and sending them back to Paris where they can have a tea party with Madam Guillotine."

Monique looked at the ground. "Have you heard anything of the marquis from the chateau?"

"Oh, yes," the soldier said. "They burned the chateau and returned all of his fancy things to the people who had worked so hard all these years. They are the true owners of France now."

"What of the marquis and his family?" asked Nanette.

"Ah, he was taken to Paris," said the guard. "I'm not sure what happened to the wife and daughter. They could be missing in the fire, but if they're out trying to escape I'm sure we'll catch them and send them to Paris to join the marquis. I'm sure he's lonely in prison without them."

Nanette squeezed Monique's hand and said nothing.

"Well, your papers look in order," he announced. "Move on. Next papers, please."

MOUNTAIN HIDEOUT, VENDÉE: JUNE 21, 1791

I continued to record Monique's life. She and Nanette had settled into life in a rebel hideout in the mountainous area of the Vendée. It was an area where many of the royalists, as well as criminals escaping justice, were hiding, but it was also a safe place for God's people to hide. The few Protestants left in France found shelter here along with some of the Catholics—those loyal to the pope *and* those loyal to God, with both of these now being a capital offense. It was a strange mix of people, yet all of them were dependent on getting along with one another.

In the year and a half Monique had been in the mountain hideout, she had become a young woman. To the human eye, she hardly resembled the child she had been when she and Nanette had escaped from the chateau. She was tall and rounded and very tan. In her peasant garb she looked and acted just like any of the other people who lived in the poverty-stricken Vendée.

"Monique," Uncle Francois called, "I need you to go into town with me today to get some supplies."

"All right," she said. "Let me tell Nanette where I am going, and I'll be right there."

Nanette exited the small hut, wiping her hands on her apron. "It's fine," she said. "Just be careful and avoid talking to anyone you don't have to. Informers are everywhere."

"Yes, I know, Nanette, and I will be careful," said Monique. "You tell me this every time we go into town, but God is taking good care of me."

Nanette nodded. "He has taken care of us," she said.

Monique smiled. She had never thought very much about God before the burning of the chateau. He had never seemed important before. Now she was learning much about Him and was even learning to read some of the scriptures that had been translated into French and brought to the Vendée by the Huguenots.

As she bumped along in the cart with Uncle Francois she heard noise coming from the village. "Something must be going on there, Uncle Francois," she said. Francois was no relation to Monique or Nanette, but in their small community they had become family and addressed each other as aunt or uncle.

"Yes," he said. "I hear shouting, and it sounds like celebrating. Maybe something good has happened."

Monique's heart lifted. Could the revolution be over? Perhaps they would all be able to go home. Maybe Papa would be out of prison, and their family could be all back together again. "Oh, please God," she whispered. "That would be wonderful."

As they rode into the village her stomach twisted into a cold knot. The people were celebrating in a frenzied, frightening way. They were doing some kind of strange dance, whirling and flailing their arms in the air, and then at the end all of them dropping to the ground as if dead.

"What are they doing?" she asked.

"Dancing," Uncle Francois replied grimly.

"Dancing?" Monique asked incredulously. "It doesn't look like any dancing I ever learned. I've never seen such a thing. It looks almost barbaric."

"It is," said Uncle Francois. "It is the carmagnole."

"Carmagnole?"

"Yes," he said. "It's the dance of the Revolution. Notice everyone drops dead in the end? I fear everyone in France will be dead before this is over. Hush now. Let us not speak of it. We are getting close to the people."

Monique stared at the dancers filling the streets. They bumped into each other as they whirled and twirled. They were wild and sweating. To her it looked more like a frenzied ritual than any fun.

They reached the first stall in the market to purchase their supplies. Uncle Francois listed their needs to the shopkeeper and then asked, "What is the celebration?"

"You haven't heard? Where have you been?" the shopkeeper retorted. "You peasants don't keep up with anything, do you?"

"Alas," Uncle Francois said, "it seems keeping up with the farm and getting enough food for the family is almost all I can do. What has happened?"

"Ah," said the shopkeeper, delighted that he could tell the story to someone who hadn't heard it. "Our foolish ex-king and that Austrian woman he had for a queen tried to escape from the Tuileries. What an idiot he is! Does he think no one would recognize him when his face is on all of our money?" He laughed crudely.

Uncle Francois tried to chuckle.

"So what happened?" Monique asked.

"Well, they made it as far as Varennes, and then they were recognized and caught and dragged back to Paris with all the indignity they deserved. They will be kept in prison now. They didn't deserve the palace at the Tuileries anyway."

"I see," Uncle Francois said, nodding his head thoughtfully.

"Yes," the shopkeeper went on, "and they've split them up now. That way they can't try to escape again as a family. And heaven knows, Louis will not try to escape without the Austrian woman, and that Austrian woman will not leave without her children, so this will probably not happen again unless they are even more foolish than we thought."

"What's going to happen to them?" Monique asked.

"I'm not sure," said the shopkeeper. "The National Assembly has not decided yet, but I hope they're all executed."

Monique turned and started carrying the supplies out to the cart. She sat out there and waited for Uncle Francois to come. She was afraid the sickness she felt in her stomach would show on her face. In a few minutes Uncle Francois joined her, and they headed toward the outside of town. The cart bumped along on the cobblestone streets. All the happiness she had felt coming into town had left her. The town that had looked so exciting and inviting now seemed cold and dirty. The chipped plaster on the battered buildings showed the wood slats beneath it.

"O God," she whispered, "I just want to go back to the mountains. At least I feel closer to You there."

They passed the large stone church on their way out of the village. Its door had been knocked off the hinges, and it stood bare and empty. The building looked as cold and unresponsive as the church it had represented.

Monique shook her head. "If I had never come to the mountains," she whispered, "I never would have learned to think of You separately from the church. But You are separate, and I'm glad I found out, because You are God, and You never change. But the church is made up of people, and some of them are good"—she glanced at Uncle Francois—"and some of them get corrupted with power." She stared back at the stone church. "Thank You for teaching me the difference."

VENDÉE MOUNTAIN HIDEOUT: SEPTEMBER 7, 1792

Uncle Francois rode into their mountain hideout and unhitched his donkey. His shoulders drooped as he led it into the cave, where he would feed it and let it rest. Nanette came out of the hut and began to unload the supplies from the cart and carry them into the back of the cave for storage. Then she stopped. "Uncle Francois," she asked, "what's the matter?"

"Something terrible has happened." Francois lifted his eyes to meet Nanette's and nodded. "There have been massacres in Paris all week," he said. "The mobs have broken into the prisons and have been killing the royal prisoners. They have killed as many aristos as they could get their hands on."

Nanette dropped her eyes. "Monique's father?" she asked.

"Yes," Uncle Francois said. "He was killed. I don't know how to tell her. I've grown so attached to that girl, I just can't bear to tell her that her papa was torn apart by a mob."

Nanette pulled herself up to her full height and squared her shoulders. "I will tell her. I've been responsible for her all of her little life. I will tell her."

Uncle Francois smiled gratefully and continued to unload the cart. Nanette turned back toward the huts.

"Monique," she called. "We must talk."

* * *

Monique sat by the mountain stream, her knees pulled up to her chest, hugging them with her arms, rocking herself slowly back and forth. She felt too numb to cry. It had been three years since she had seen her papa, but when she had found out that he was not killed when the chateau was burned, she had always imagined that somehow he would get out of prison and come find her. "Now that will never happen," she whispered.

Uncle Francois walked up behind her. "Monique, ma petite." She turned to look at him. The older man dropped his eyes. As fond as he was of Monique, he couldn't help remembering that she was the daughter of a marquis.

"I am sorry about your papa," he said. Monique nodded, unable to talk.

"I . . . I brought you something," he stammered. Reaching into the large pocket of his billowing peasant smock, he pulled out a small slip of paper. "It's a Scripture piece. This one you may keep. It's yours." He turned and fled back to the cluster of huts.

Monique held it in her hand for a long time just looking at the water. Finally she opened it. There, inscribed in French in Uncle Francois' shaky handwriting was a copy of a Scripture verse: "I will be a father to the fatherless."

Big tears welled in Monique's eyes and poured down her cheeks. "Oh, thank You, God," she whispered. "How good You are to send me a message like this right now. You've been my Father for the last three years, and You've taken good care of me. You've protected me and fed me. Oh, thank You."

She clutched the scrap of paper tightly in her hand until she realized it was all crumpled and soaked with perspiration. Reaching inside her ragged dress, she unpinned a tiny locket from the lining of her chemise. Nanette had sold all of her jewelry she had been wearing the day they escaped, except for her tiny locket. She popped it open and looked again at the miniature portrait of her mother and father, then she folded Uncle Francois' scrap of paper into a tiny piece, fit it into the center of the locket, and pinned it back inside her undergarment. "You are the only papa I have now," she whispered, "but You are a good one, and I love You."

I smiled. The trees around the mountain stream rustled as the Spirit of the Almighty drew close. He caressed Monique's face with a cool breeze and dried her tears into little clean paths down her dusty face. I nodded my head, even though she couldn't see me. Monique was right. He was the best Father she would ever have.

VANDÉE HIDEOUT: DECEMBER 25, 1792

Monique clutched her ragged blanket around her shoulders as she stirred the water in the huge caldron over the open fire. Uncle Francois limped out of his cave, where he and two of the other men slept with the donkey. "Come sit by the fire, Uncle Francois," Monique called. "Perhaps if you get warm, your joints won't hurt you so badly."

Uncle Francois nodded and limped over to the log she had rolled up for him.

"Thank you, ma petite. Joyeux noel."

Monique caught her breath. That's right, today was Christmas. "Happy birthday, Jesus," she whispered.

Uncle Francois smiled. "You talk to Him a lot, don't you?"

"Oh, did I say that out loud?" Monique said, embarrassed.

Uncle Francois nodded. "It's good, ma petite," he said. "Talk to Him all you want to. It's a good thing."

I nodded. It *was* a good thing. Monique spoke with the Almighty more and more often as she grew older and as times grew harder.

"Would you like a nice hot drink?" she asked.

Uncle Francois laughed. "I suppose that means we're out of porridge and we're just going to drink hot water this morning?"

Monique nodded. The last time Uncle Francois had gone to the village for supplies, the man who usually helped them was gone, and his small shop was all broken and empty. No one knew where he was. The food had run out the day before.

"Well," Monique explained, "I put some water on to boil anyway, because with this cold, drinking something hot will at least warm your insides."

Uncle Francois smiled at her. "A hot drink sounds good," he said. "It won't hurt any of us to go without food for a few days. The Lord knows we're here, and He will take care of us."

I hope You don't forget us here, Monique thought. *You knew my papa was in prison too.* Then she shook her head. "I can't be thinking things like that," she said. "I'm going to have to just trust You to take care of us. Someday maybe I will understand why some of these things have happened. Until then I need just to trust You."

She ladled out a mug of the hot water, and Uncle Francois cupped it in his gnarled hands.

"Do you hear horses?" asked Monique.

Uncle Francois cocked his head. His hearing was not as sharp as Monique's. "Quick," he said, "to the cave. It *is* horses."

"I will not leave you," Monique said, and she sat down resolutely on the log next to Uncle Francois.

Two men rode into the clearing. They looked like soldiers. Monique slipped her hand into Uncle Francois' gnarled one and tried to keep from shaking.

"Ho, anybody up?" one of them shouted. Nanette rushed out of her hut. The other two men emerged from the cave.

"We're up," Uncle Francois shouted.

"We are traveling and hungry," said the soldier. "What do you have in your pot there?"

"Hot water," Monique answered. "We haven't started to fix breakfast yet."

The two men got off their horses. "We'll wait," they stated.

"Well, you'll wait a long time," Nanette said. "We have no breakfast. This young optimist here has made us hot water because she thinks it will keep us warmer than cold water, but we have no food."

The soldiers looked at each other. "But you know how to cook, don't you?" one asked Monique.

"Oh, yes," Monique answered. She had learned to make bread, stew, and everything that Nanette knew how to cook.

"Well," one of the soldiers said, "we have a few things in our bag here. If you'll throw them in the pot, we'll go hunting and see if we can find something in these woods." They took a small bag off the back of one of the horses and tossed it to Monique. They remounted their horses and left.

Monique opened the bag. Where had they found these things? "Look, Nanette," she cried. "Carrots, turnips, and potatoes!"

Monique stared after the men. "Where are they from?" she asked. "They must be important if they have food rations like this!" There were also two loaves of bread. Quickly she and Nanette cut up the vegetables and threw them in the pot. In a short time the men were back from their hunting with a large stag. Expertly they butchered the deer and gave some of the meat to Monique to put in the stew pot. The rest of it they cut in strips. They packed it between layers of snow next to Nanette's hut.

"There," one of them grunted. "The snow should keep the meat fresh, and you will have meat for several weeks if you're careful. Now, is that stew ready yet?"

Uncle Francois sat chuckling by the fire. The warmth had helped his joints, and he didn't seem to be in pain anymore. He patted Monique's arm as she handed him a mug of hot soup.

"I told you He would provide," he said. "He wouldn't invite us to His birthday party without some food."

Monique laughed too. It was a good Christmas after all.

VENDÉE MOUNTAIN HIDEOUT: JANUARY 1793

Uncle Francois rode into camp and stiffly climbed out of his cart. The others rushed over to him. "What's the news from the village?" Nanette demanded.

"Well," Uncle Francois said, "there is no food in the village either."

Monique started to laugh. "Uncle Francois, you won't believe what we found."

He looked at her and raised one eyebrow. She always laughed when he did this. "What did you find, Monique?" he asked.

"You remember when you invited those soldiers to sleep in the cave with you and the other men? Well, Nanette and I were cleaning it out and putting new straw in there for you men and the donkey to sleep on, and we found another whole bag of root vegetables. They left us a whole bag! Look at all of these!" She dragged the bag out of Nanette's hut.

"God is good," Uncle Francois said fervently.

"Yes," Monique agreed, "and so were those soldiers. And to think we were afraid of them! They must not have known we were fugitives."

Uncle Francois raised one eyebrow again. "Of course they knew we were fugitives. Why would we be hiding in little huts and caves in the mountain instead of living in the village like normal people?"

Everyone in the group stopped and stared at each other. "Do you think they will denounce us?"

"I doubt it," said Nanette. "They gave us food, and we cooked for them." The group was very quiet.

Uncle Francois limped over to the log by the fire and sat down carefully. "Well, I don't suppose you want to know the rest of the news of what's going on in France."

"Oh, tell us," Monique cried. Everyone clustered around Uncle Francois.

"It's not good," Uncle Francois said. "We may as well talk about the soldiers denouncing us."

"Oh, give us the news, you old pessimist," Nanette urged gruffly.

"King Louis was executed this week in Paris. France is being ruled by the Committee of Public Safety, which apparently it is not. It is headed by a man named Robespierre."

Monique sucked in her breath. "Oh. Papa always said that Robespierre was a hot-headed idiot."

"Oui," Uncle Francois agreed. "He seems to be hot-headed anyway. The Committee of Public Safety has ordered hundreds of executions. It has set up a guillotine in the square in Paris, and people sit around for entertainment and watch the executions. All of the executioners are competing to see who can perform more executions in less time. The record is currently being held by one man who was able to cut off 32 heads in 25 minutes. Apparently that's not fast enough for the Committee of Public Safety, for word has it that they even drilled holes in the bottom of barges filled with condemned aristos and their families and sank them in the rivers."

Everyone was silent, shaking their heads. They were cold in the mountains. They got tired of what little food they had sometimes, and a few times they had been hungry. But surely this was better than living in Paris under the Reign of Terror that Robespierre was leading.

"There is more," Uncle Francois went on. "Morally we are atheists now as a country. We worship the Goddess of Reason. They took a young street woman—"

"Shh, not in front of Monique," Nanette growled.

Uncle Francois just looked at her, "—and dressed her up in robes and named her the Goddess of Reason. Everyone was bowing and worshiping her. They were burning crucifixes and in some churches just draping the colors of the Revolution over the body of Jesus. Still others had big plaques reading 'Crush the Wretch.' The Bible has been banned, the church has been banned, and the bishop of Paris was led out in front of everyone to worship the Goddess of Reason, and he did." Everyone shook their heads.

"Mon Dieu," Nanette prayed, "what has happened to our

country? They have turned their backs on You. And You have turned Your back on them too. Will anyone be left alive in France?" The little group sat in silence.

"O God," Monique whispered, "please be merciful to my country. A few of us here still love You."

The guardians drew close to comfort them, and I hovered nearby, feeling helpless. How does one comfort the sorrow brought by humans choosing sin rather than the life the Almighty wanted to give them? Surely even the Almighty wept.

VENDÉE MOUNTAIN HIDEOUT: JUNE 1794

"We're out of food again," Monique said to Nanette. "You must let me take my locket into the village and sell it."

"No," Nanette protested. "You may not. First of all, when they see that piece of jewelry they will know you are an aristo. Aristos are the only ones selling jewelry for food now. And secondly there's no food in the village to buy, even if you did get gold for your locket. Whom would we buy it from? It is summertime. We will find something in the woods, or the Lord will provide; besides, you must keep that one piece. You may need it some day for identification to prove who you are."

Monique snorted. "Who am I? What am I going to prove? My papa is dead. He was executed as an enemy of France. I have no family except you."

"You will keep it," said Nanette firmly.

Monique pinned the locket back inside her chemise. There was no talking sense to Nanette sometimes. She shrugged, "Well, then let me get a basket and come with you to the woods. Maybe the Lord will tell us where He's been hiding the things that are good to eat there."

Nanette laughed. "He always does, Monique," she said. "He's very good to us."

Monique nodded.

When they returned to camp, there was excitement in the air. Uncle Francois looked as if he were about to burst. "Sit down, ma petite and Miss Nanette. I must speak with you."

Obediently they set down their heavy basket and focused on Uncle Francois.

"The Lord was very good to us out in the woods today," Monique said. "We found lots of roots."

Uncle Francois grinned. "The Lord has been very good today," he said. "Wait till you hear what I have to tell you." He paused for effect. "Monique, your maman is alive. She didn't die when the chateau burned."

Monique felt as if she could not breathe. "Where is she? Is she all right? The Committee hasn't caught her, has it?"

Uncle Francois chortled with glee. "I met with one of my contacts today," he said. No one ever asked Uncle Francois who his contacts were. It was safer not to know. "Your maman escaped the burning chateau and was helped across the Channel by some Royalist supporters. She is living in England and has been saving. Now she has enough money for you to come join her. And she has sent for you."

Monique felt the blood draining from her face. She had a family! She had Maman.

"Quick!" Uncle Francois shouted. "Somebody catch her! The girl is going to faint!" Strong arms lowered her down onto the log next to Uncle Francois.

"Here, have a drink of water," Nanette urged.

Slowly everything came back into focus, and Monique started laughing hysterically. "I have a maman! I have a maman!" She flung her arms around Nanette. "Nanette, you have been a wonderful maman to me. You have taken good care of me, but isn't it wonderful my maman is alive! What will I do? My maman will think I'm a heretic now. I read Scriptures. I don't go to confession. I haven't been to Mass in years."

Uncle Francois put his arm around her. "Don't be afraid, little one," he said. "If the Lord has found your maman and has helped our contacts get the message through, don't be afraid to go to her. They don't burn heretics in England these days."

"They don't?"

"No," he said. "Right now heretics are as welcome in England as Catholics are. And who knows what your maman believes now? She's been through some hard times too. The contacts say it took her two years from the burning of the chateau to escape to England."

Monique nodded. The hard times had changed her. They had changed Nanette. Perhaps they had changed Maman too.

SHIP ON THE ENGLISH CHANNEL: JULY 1794

Monique stood at the rail, staring at the cliffs in the distance, the crashing waves splashing the salty spray in her face. "What if Maman does not recognize me?" she asked Nanette. "I've changed a lot. What if . . . what if she doesn't want me when she finds out that I'm a heretic? What if . . . what if . . . ?"

"Oh, hush!" Nanette scolded. "Maman wants you, or she would not have sent for you and sent money for your passage to England. And God wants you to go to your maman, or He would not have helped us escape safely from the Vendée to Calais and cross the Channel safely. Look, we're almost there."

And they were. Nanette was right. The two women had no clue how much work they had been for the guardians in the last two weeks. Monique clutched Nanette's hand. "I love you, Nanette," she murmured.

"And I you," the older woman answered with tears in her eyes.

"It was hard to leave Uncle Francois and the others, but I just couldn't have done this if you weren't coming with me."

"Oh, la child," snorted Nanette in her brusque way. "I have been with you since the night you were born. This is hardly the time for me to go my own way."

The two women clung to each other as they peered into the mist ahead. On the dock was another woman clad in black, every bit as anxious.

With Nanette close behind, Monique followed the captain down the gangplank and approached the woman in black. "Madam," he said, "I believe I have the guests you requested."

She nodded and handed him a small bag of gold coins. "And here is the reward I promised," she said. The captain withdrew, and they were left alone.

The woman in black pushed back her hood, her dark hair pulled back into a severe bun. Her eyes were dark, and her face was lined. She wore no makeup.

"Monique," she asked, "is it you?"

Monique stared at the woman. "Yes," she answered.

"Oh, you have changed so much," she said. "The day the chateau burned, you were a little girl. I thought you had died in the fire. I grieved for you so." Her eyes filled with tears.

"Maman?" asked Monique.

The lady nodded.

"But you don't look like Maman. What happened to your hair? It used to be so tall and white."

Maman laughed. "Yes, we wore powdered wigs there," she said. "And lots of powder and paint on our faces, but this is who I was underneath all of that."

Monique started to laugh. "And what are you wearing? Where are the bright-colored velvets and brocades you always wore, the deep plunging necklines that hardly covered your bosom, and the strings of diamonds?"

Maman laughed. "You're hardly a Paris fashion yourself."

Monique looked down at her ragged dress and the cloak she had made out of the tattered blanket. She shrugged. "I don't care about clothes," she said. "I'm alive."

Maman laughed. "Yes, me too. Many things have changed since we saw each other last, and I just pray you will understand, Monique."

"You pray?" Monique queried.

Maman stared at her hard. Nanette stared at both of them.

"I . . . I had to learn English here," said Maman, "and I learned to read English. People have the whole Bible in English here. That child of Queen Mary of Scotland who was married to the dauphin of France so long ago—her son, King James, I believe his name was, had the Bible all translated into English. It's everywhere here. Anyone can read it. It's very interesting."

Monique caught her breath. "You read Scriptures?" she asked.

"Yes, I do. I hope you're not disappointed in me, but I think if you read them too, you would—"

"Maman, I do!" squealed Monique. "I've been reading Scripture passages in the Vendée, in our little mountain hideout."

They grabbed and hugged each other.

I chuckled in spite of myself. I knew this all along, but this was one part of my job that was fun!

Maman turned to Nanette. "Oh, Nanette," she said. "I'm so sorry for the way I sometimes treated you in the old days. Thank you so much for saving my daughter and taking such good care of her. You must come live with us. You will be part of our family. You won't be a servant anymore. I can't afford them. But you can be Aunt Nanette." The three women hugged each other and burst into tears.

And I smiled. The guardians were all standing around with big grins on their faces, looking proud of themselves. And so they should. Working for the Almighty is something to be proud of.

EPILOGUE

Monique's maman had married an Englishman, and they were able to arrange a very good marriage for Monique too. Nanette went with Monique to her new home and helped Monique raise her children. They called her Grandma Nanette.

Monique and Maman were horrified as they learned of more and more friends and relatives being executed during the Reign of Terror. Robespierre was executed by his own people, as were many others. Finally in 1795 the Reign of Terror ended.

France had been practically crippled by her revolution. It seemed ironic to me that the members of the aristocracy had been dragged out kicking and screaming and executed on the very spot where so many of God's followers had been executed 200 years before that. Surely this was an example to the whole world of how terrible life could be in a country that turned its back totally on God.

King Louis XVI had been executed, and the next year his queen, Marie Antoinette, had died under the blade too. As for Monique's young cousin, Louis the dauphin, his whereabouts never became known to Monique or Maman. The last they had heard, he had been in prison. There will be a time, though, when all those questions will be answered.

Meanwhile, Monique and her maman and Grandma Nanette had the opportunity to listen to the teachings of preachers John and Charles Wesley in England. Maman got to meet John Wesley before he died, and she become very fond of the hymns he and his brother had written. She and Monique, as well as Nanette and their families, joined the Methodist Church that the two brothers had founded, and they continued to learn more about the Scriptures and more about how passionately the Most High loved them. Even when Monique was a very old woman, her favorite song was still one of the Charles Wesley tunes: "Jesus, Lover of My Soul."

It always made the guardians and me smile when we heard her singing it from her rocking chair, for truly He was the lover of her soul.

RACHEL

U.S.A., A.D. 1843-1849

WASHINGTON, NEW HAMPSHIRE: 1843

y assignment now was to record the choices and events in the life of a little girl named Rachel who lived on the east coast of the New World country called the United States. Her family was fairly successful, her father being the chief reporter for a local newspaper. Rachel and her mother attended the Methodist church, and so did Papa on special occasions like Christmas and Easter—and for funerals or weddings of importance.

"Rachel," Mama called. "Come set this plate of corn on the table and then call your papa and tell him dinner is ready."

Rachel breathed in deeply. She loved the smell of hot, buttered corn. Carefully setting the heavy plate on the table, she ran to the study.

"Papa," she called. "Dinner is finally ready."

Papa looked up from his writing and wiped the tip of his pen. He chuckled. "You are always hungry, my little one, aren't you?"

"Well, right now anyway," Rachel said. "Aren't you?"

"Yes," Papa agreed. "Let's go eat." He wiped his hands carefully on his handkerchief.

Rachel giggled in spite of herself. Papa was always careful to wipe his pen before putting it away and wiping his hands, but as usual he had a big ink smear across the side of his nose and onto his cheek. Mama said that writers had ink in their blood and they were happiest when they had it all over them too. Rachel wasn't sure about the first part, for when Papa cut his finger he pretty much bled like anyone else, but he did have ink on him most of the time.

As they ate their dinner Mama asked, "So what is the big story you're working on this week?"

"William Miller," said Papa. "Have you heard of him?"

"Yes," said Mama. "He has been giving lectures all along the east coast in different homes and a few churches. I believe his farm isn't far from our home."

"That's true," said Papa. "He lives in Low Hampton, New York. He has published a series of his lectures in book form. I have been reviewing it for the paper, and I would like to attend one of his meetings. Would you like to come along? You two usually seem interested in all that religious stuff."

"Yes," said Mama, "we would."

The next day at school Rachel sat on the steps with her best friend, Uriah. The other boys played ball after eating their lunches, but Uriah had never been able to walk properly as long as Rachel had known him. He had been treated with calomel for something when he was a very little boy, and it had left his left leg covered with ulcers and crippled. The ulcers seemed to be getting worse, and Uriah had a hard time walking around. He and Rachel had become very close friends and would sit on the steps and talk every day at lunchtime.

"Papa is taking us to hear William Miller speak this weekend," Rachel announced.

"Really?" Uriah asked. "I heard he has a mental condition and is a little out of touch."

Rachel laughed. "Oh, that's what they say about anybody different," she said. "Papa has a copy of his book because he had to write about him for the paper. He might let us borrow it if you would like to look at it."

"Sure," said Uriah. "I am interested in how mentally ill people think."

Rachel laughed. Uriah was a big tease, but Rachel knew he loved books and would be eager to read anything before forming his final opinion. "I'll ask Papa if I can bring it tomorrow," she said. "Papa says that William Miller believes that Jesus is going to come sometime in the next couple years, and then the end of the world will be here."

"H'mm. That perspective has to be a little distressing for some."

Rachel nodded. "I suppose so," she said. "I think that I would be very happy to see Him, though."

"You and me both." Uriah looked down at his leg. "I'd be happy for Him to come this afternoon, so I could trade in this leg for one that actually worked. Then you'd have to read books by yourself at noon, because I might have to play ball."

Rachel laughed. "I believe if you had two perfect legs you would still talk to me at lunchtime," she said.

Uriah blushed and then mumbled something like "Yeah, maybe."

Rachel was right. Her papa didn't mind her borrowing the book. He was finished with it. She carried the heavy tome to school with her, anxious to share it with Uriah. But Uriah didn't show up. His sister, Annie, was there, though, and when the teacher finally let them out for lunch, Rachel rushed over to her.

"Annie, where is Uriah? Why isn't he here today?"

Annie turned her blue eyes to the younger girl. "His leg is

worse," she said. "The ulcers are becoming more and more infected. Mama had the doctor come last night because Uriah was crying with the pain. He's given him some new medicine, but he said if the ulcers don't improve soon, they're going to have to take his leg."

"Take his leg?" queried Rachel. "You mean cut it off?"

Annie nodded.

"Won't that kill him?"

"I don't know," Annie answered. "Maybe. It sounds awful, but the doctor says he might die if they don't."

Rachel felt as if someone had kicked her in the stomach. "Please take this book home to him," she said, "if he feels well enough to read. And tell him I'm praying for him."

Annie smiled. "I'll do that, Rachel," she said. "Uriah is practically out of his mind with the pain and his fever right now, but it will mean a lot that you care for him so much."

Rachel wandered over to the steps and sat silently where she and Uriah usually sat at lunchtime. "Dear God," she prayed, "please let William Miller be right, and let Jesus come quickly, like maybe tonight, so that Uriah's leg won't hurt anymore, and please don't let my friend die."

* * *

The next day and the next, Rachel looked for Annie and Uriah at school but neither were there. She couldn't stand the suspense any longer, and the minute the school bell rang at the end of the day she hurried to the Smiths' house. She had to know what was happening.

As she approached the front porch she could hear low moaning coming from the upstairs bedroom. It made the knot in her stomach feel worse. She stood and listened for a moment, then she timidly tapped on the door.

Annie came to the door and slipped out onto the porch. She

looked terrible. She had dark circles under her eyes, and her hair was limp and stringy. "Rachel," she said, "come sit down."

"Uriah is worse?" she asked.

Annie nodded. "The doctor took his leg yesterday," she said.

"They cut it off?"

"Yes," said Annie.

"Did it hurt him?" Rachel asked.

Annie rubbed her hands together slowly. "It was awful," she said. "Several of us had to hold him down, and the doctor just cut it off. He's been given something now to help him sleep, but the pain must just be unimaginable. I imagine I can still hear his screaming."

Rachel's eyes filled with tears. "Is he going to be OK?" she asked.

"I don't know," Annie said. "We're praying hard that he will be. It depends whether his leg heals or whether the infection still spreads."

"Let's pray for him now," Rachel whispered. The two girls held hands and prayed for the boy they both cared about.

I wished they could see the guardians pulling close over his bed and bringing rest to the fevered boy. The Almighty had already shared with us that He had serious plans for this child, but for now Rachel and Annie would just have to trust.

* * *

"Oh, Annie," cried Rachel. "The meetings were good. I wish you could have come with me. Mr. Miller is quite a Bible scholar. He has things all figured out from Daniel and Revelation and all those confusing books with all those numbers and beasts and everything, and it just makes so much sense when he explains it."

"Explain it to me," Annie begged.

"I can't," Rachel said. "I don't really understand all the math, except that when he preached it, I really believed it, and I am just sure that Jesus is coming soon."

"Did he say exactly when?" Annie asked. "It would be so nice to know when."

"No, he just said sometime around 1843."

"But that's now. It could be anytime now."

"Oh, that would be wonderful!" Annie exclaimed.

"How is Uriah doing?" asked Rachel.

"He's getting better," said Annie. "I gave him your book, and he glanced at it a little, although he is still quite tired and weak from his operation. And he still sleeps a lot from the laudanum the doctor gave him for pain, but I'm going to start reading it to him when he's awake. Uriah is such an intellectual. He will really enjoy that stuff, and he'll probably understand the math."

The two girls laughed. I chuckled. Uriah would understand the math, and he would enjoy the book. I knew that it would be only a matter of weeks before the entire Smith family would become as excited about the Lord's coming as Rachel was.

The band of Millerites was growing so fast that William Miller was no longer the only speaker. Many speakers were traveling and spreading the word. And the little group of believers had grown to 50,000. Many were considered fanatics and were disfellowshipped from the churches they belonged to. Yet with the prospect of Jesus' coming and taking them home soon, they were able to take these things in stride and were filled with joy and anticipation.

ASCENSION ROCK, MILLER'S FARM: OCTOBER 22, 1844

"Papa, Papa, wake up! Today is the day Jesus is coming!"

"It isn't even morning yet," Papa groaned.

"Sure it is," Rachel said. "It's just not light, but we don't want to be late. What if He comes at the crack of dawn?"

"It's possible. God is an early riser, you know. All of His creatures seem to be. Then there is the owl and the bat and—"

"Oh, Papa," Rachel scolded. "Come on. You said you would take me over to the Millers' farm today."

"Yes, I did," Papa said. "Go get ready, and your mother and I will be down soon."

Rachel scampered back to her room. Jesus was coming today! What more could anybody possibly want? She pulled on her clothes and ran downstairs.

Mama was excited too. Papa said he was coming along only to cover the story for the newspaper. "I'll drive you two as far as Mr. Miller's farm," he promised. "The Lord will have to take you the rest of the way. He knows I'm pretty much just a New Hampshire boy."

"Oh, come on, Papa. Come with us!" they cried.

"I'll stay with you at Miller's farm and see what happens," Papa promised.

Rachel and Mama had been praying and praying that Papa would be ready and want to go to heaven with them, but so far he insisted he was there just to cover the news.

"Well, that's good," Mama said. "The Lord is going to give him some pretty amazing stuff to cover."

It was not yet light when they reached Miller's farm, but it was already crowded. Papa found a place to unhitch the horse while Mama and Rachel walked through the crowds looking for friends.

Out near the big, flat rock on Miller's farm, Rachel found Annie and Uriah. "I'm so glad you two could get here early," she said. "This is going to be just wonderful."

"Yes," Uriah answered. "I wouldn't miss it for anything. After all, I'm waiting for my new leg!" They all laughed.

"It's good to see you up and around, Uriah," Rachel said. He smiled.

I felt a deep heaviness as I hovered near the children. They were so excited, so joyful to be seeing their King soon. Already I was feeling the pain they would soon be feeling. Would they be able to rise above it? Would these young ones be able to understand why William Miller was allowed to have misunderstood this prophecy? I didn't know. The guardians looked anxious too and were gathered in large numbers. Their services were not needed yet, but they would be shortly, and the guardians were ready.

"I'm glad to be up and around again too," Uriah said. "Although if Jesus had come last summer when we first thought He might, I would still have two legs."

"Aw, you'll have another one by tonight," Annie teased. "When you look back after five or six thousand years, one year without a leg won't seem like much."

"That's true," laughed Uriah. "In the perspective of eternity I guess one human year is really not much."

I nodded, even though they couldn't see me. One human year wasn't much, but I also knew that to these young people, one human year could seem like an eternity.

The little group sang and prayed. Some were anxious and tearful, searching their minds for any unconfessed sins they might have. Others were too excited at the prospect of seeing their King to spend any time in tears.

The day wore on. As those awaiting Christ's return watched and waited, sang and visited, Rachel's father worked his way through the crowd, chatting and making notes. Occasionally he looked nervously toward the sky. He was not a believer, but occasionally he wondered what would happen if Jesus really did come that day. I could tell his heart was torn between hoping nothing would happen to confirm his stand on the issue and hoping that his wife and daughter would not be ridiculed and disappointed.

Already there had been division in every church that the

Millerite message had been preached. Those who loved the Almighty were thrilled at the thought of seeing Him soon, while those who did not love Him as much as they professed were not interested in seeing Him any time in the near future. Not only did they show a lack of excitement over the prospect of His coming, but they opposed those who were spreading the good news.

There were stories of those who had been disfellowshipped from their churches. One young Millerite had been encouraged and thrilled at the idea of Jesus' soon coming, and she spoke her testimony in a meeting and gave Jesus the glory for relieving her depression and giving her such encouragement.

The minister said, "And this encouragement was brought about by your belief in Methodism?"

"No," she said. "It's not Methodism. It's not because I'm a Methodist. This is because Jesus is coming soon." The minister was so angry that she was disfellowshipped from the church and had to worship with others like her in local homes.

The guardians and I were horrified at the lack of respect shown for our King and for those who loved Him by the very people who claimed to be His shepherds. I knew that no matter how bad it had been before today, tomorrow would be worse.

Rachel's father was talking to Mr. Hastings, a farmer from New Ipswitch. "Well, sir," he said, "my potatoes are still in the ground. I saw no point in using my precious time to dig them up, when I'm going to be eating at Christ's table for dinner. Besides, the crops were disappointing to those who did harvest theirs this year. The potato blight has been terrible. Almost all the potatoes in our community were of very poor quality and of no use at all, and while we would use what we could in our homes, they wouldn't be sellable. I'd much rather go to heaven and eat ambrosia and fruit from the tree of life. I don't care what it is—anything will be better than blighted potatoes anyhow."

Rachel's father laughed. "But what if Jesus doesn't come today?"

Mr. Hastings shrugged. "I haven't even devoted time to that thought," he confided. "He is coming, and I am going home. Who wants to worry about what if's?"

Rachel's father nodded, made a few more notes in his book, and moved on to the next person. He had enough material for several feature articles already. Today had been very good for business. He glanced at the sky again. Red streaks with bands of blue and gold made a beautiful picture, but it was just the sunset. Soon darkness fell, and still Jesus had not come.

* * *

It was past midnight, yet the 10-year-old still tossed in her bed. Finally she got up and walked to the window to look out at the stars. "Why didn't You come, Jesus? We loved You so much. We were so excited to see You. Did You forget us?"

As her glance lowered she realized a light was shining out from the window of the parlor downstairs. Wiping her eyes, she went to investigate. The stairs creaked as she padded down in her bare feet. Opening the door to the parlor, she discovered Papa. He was sitting at the desk writing. He turned to face his little daughter, noting her blotchy face and red swollen eyes.

"You're up awfully late, sweetheart," he said.

"I couldn't sleep, Papa," Rachel answered.

Papa smiled sympathetically. "It was a hard day for you and your mama."

Rachel nodded. "I don't understand what happened," she said. "How could He have forgotten us? Did we not understand the prophecy right, or does He just not love us?"

"Not love you?" said Papa. "Of course He loves you." His tone was much sharper than he intended, and he reached out and scooped his daughter close in his arms. "How could He not love you?" he whispered. "You're one of His most loyal followers. Any God who would disappoint you like that is not worth following, in my opinion."

I watched silently. While his words were harsh, I knew that he was still filled with indecision, weighing one side against the other. And his words were influenced more by his protective anger over his daughter's broken heart than true hostility toward the Almighty. God would understand that even better than I, for He too is protective of the feelings of His children, and His heart was breaking along with theirs at their sadness. The other recorders and I had carefully kept track of every insult and every indignity that His friends had experienced while waiting for Him to come, and we were going to continue, for He plans to make it up to them.

"Papa," Rachel asked. "Do you suppose the disciples felt like this the night after Jesus was crucified?"

Papa looked down at her in surprise. "I . . . I . . . well, I suppose so," he admitted. "They would have been very shocked and disappointed. Weren't they expecting Him to be crowned King instead?"

"Um-hmm," Rachel said. "Maybe we just didn't understand what was happening here. Maybe things happened according to God's plan, and we just misunderstood what the plan was."

Papa smoothed his hair with his inky hands. "Perhaps," he said, "or perhaps not, but whatever the case, you know that I love you, Rachel."

"I love you too, Papa," she said.

"Now go back to bed, honey. I have to have an article ready for the paper in the morning. And I'll be writing a lot on this. I'm going to go back to New Ipswitch in a couple of days and find that farmer, Mr. Hastings, who never harvested his potatoes. I want to see what he has to say now, and I may be doing some other traveling through New England for some feature articles on this. If you want to go with me, I'm sure your mama could spare you for a few days, and you could find out what some of the other Millerites are thinking. Would you like that?"

"Oh, yes," Rachel answered. "I really would. Maybe somebody will be able to explain some of this so that it makes some sense."

"Maybe," Papa said, "if anything about the Millerite movement made any sense. In the meantime, you get some sleep, and I'll finish this article."

Rachel hugged her papa again and headed back upstairs. Her guardian hovered close and covered her with his wings so that the cloud of depression hovering in her room couldn't touch her. And she fell into an exhausted slumber.

WASHINGTON, nEW HAMPSHIRE: nOVEMBER 1, 1844

"Hey, Uriah," Rachel called as she ran toward the house.

"I'm out here on the front porch," Uriah shouted back.

Rachel rounded the corner and slowed to a more dignified walk. "I brought you something," she said.

"Really?" said Uriah. "From New Ipswitch?"

"Yes."

"What is it?" Uriah asked, reaching out his hand. Rachel pulled a large potato from the pocket of her dress and held it out to him. "It looks like a potato," said the 16-year-old.

"I always knew you were a genius," Rachel said, giggling.

"That's never been in question," Uriah teased. "But tell me, is this a special potato?"

"Well, look at it," Rachel advised.

Uriah turned it over and over in his hands. It was a very large potato, and it looked like a healthy one. "This potato is from New Ipswitch?" he asked.

"Yes."

"I give up," he said. "Tell me what's special about this potato."

"Well, a genius you may be," Rachel observed, "but a farmer you're not."

Uriah nodded. "So?"

"Remember Papa's article last week in the paper?"

"Yes," said Uriah. "I think your papa believes we're a bunch of fools."

"Well, my papa is a kind man. It's just that he's a reporter and he works for a newspaper that isn't very sympathetic to us Millerites. But remember what he said about Mr. Hastings and how he hadn't dug up any of his potatoes? This is a Hastings potato."

"Aw," commented Uriah. "So I have a nice, respectable Millerite potato here."

Rachel laughed. "Oh, it's more than that. Remember in the article that Papa said all the potato crops up and down New England had the blight?"

"Oh, that's right," Uriah said, as understanding dawned across his face.

I couldn't help chuckling. These humans are so amusing to watch, especially when they have just caught on.

Uriah lit up with a huge smile now. "I don't see much blight on this one. This is probably the most enormous potato in New England, and it's healthy-looking too."

"Exactly," Rachel said. "Mr. Hastings and his family went out and dug up their potato crop after the Disappointment last week. It gave them something to do instead of sitting home feeling miserable as we did. All of his potatoes are like this. He gave Papa a whole huge bag of them to bring home. Papa put one on the desk of everybody at the newspaper office, and Mama has been fixing them for us at home. We're going to have some for dinner. We're going to have the most wonderful potatoes in all of New England. Jesus may not have come last week, and Mr. Hastings may have been late in harvesting his potatoes, but God protected his potatoes from the blight. Look at them! Aren't they awesome?"

Uriah nodded slowly. "God is really good. We must have misunderstood something."

"Well, you know," Rachel said, "I've been thinking about this, and there have been people in the Bible who didn't understand what was going on either. Job couldn't figure out why he was having such a hard time, and God didn't hold that against him for not understanding. Job just always insisted that God was good no matter how confusing things were. And that's what I'm going to do. I don't understand what happened last week, and I don't understand why Jesus didn't come and get us, but I believe God is good, and I'm just going to have to hang onto that."

Uriah nodded. "You make a lot of sense for a little 10-year-old," he said.

I smiled too. It wouldn't be the first time that a younger person had been used to strengthen the faith of others. And Rachel was right. The Almighty counts loyalty among His followers much higher than intellectual gymnastics and being able to explain every single thing.

FAIR HAVEN, MASSACHUSETTS: FALL 1846

"Papa, I'm glad you let me come with you on this trip," Rachel said.

"Well," Papa answered, "with everything that has happened, I think it's good for you to be exposed to these different religious beliefs. Then you can decide for yourself whether you really believe any of this stuff or not. And besides, I enjoy the company."

"It would be fun to meet Captain Bates," Rachel said.

"Yes," Papa added. "I heard he was in Washington not too long ago. He came and met with Frederick Wheeler and Silas Farnsworth."

"Oh, the two Sabbathkeepers."

"Yes, he wanted to learn more about the Sabbath. If he was learning about the Sabbath from Mr. Wheeler and Mr. Farnsworth right here in our own town, why did we come here to Fair Haven?"

Papa laughed. "Nobody in town is going to want to read a story about what Mr. Wheeler or Mr. Farnsworth believe. They're just neighbors. But if you do a story on someone out of town, especially someone as rich as Captain Bates, then it's news!"

Rachel laughed. "Well, whatever the reason," she said, "I'm glad I got to come with you. This must be their house."

Papa drew the buggy to a stop and tied the horses to a hitching post. I watched as Rachel's father knocked on the door and introduced himself. Mrs. Bates politely invited them in, though the captain was out on an errand and would be back soon. But she invited them into the parlor and served them some lemonade.

"I'd like to introduce you to our guests here," said Mrs. Bates. "This is James and Ellen White. They got married earlier this year."

"Well, congratulations," Papa said. Rachel smiled.

"James and Ellen have been traveling and doing some preaching with the Advent movement," Mrs. Bates announced.

"Oh, really," Papa said, his reporter antenna shooting up.

"Why, yes. In fact, Ellen had a vision right after the Great Disappointment a couple years ago, and she's been sharing that with other Advent people. Tell us about it, Ellen," encouraged Mrs. Bates.

Ellen looked at the floor. She seemed very shy. "I will," she said.

Rachel felt sorry for her. She had never had problems with being shy, so she spoke up to make Ellen more comfortable. "I'm 12," she said, "so I'm old enough to go with my dad on some of his trips. How old are you?"

"I'm 18," said Ellen.

Papa nudged Rachel. "Honey, you never ask a woman her age," he whispered.

"Oh," said Rachel. "Sorry."

Ellen smiled. "I really don't mind," she said, now putting Rachel at ease. "And James is 25. And he's not a lady, so you're allowed to ask."

James chuckled.

"I guess not," Papa admitted.

James was tall and lanky and very skinny. He didn't look very strong, and he walked with a bit of a limp. *Perhaps he hurt his ankle when he was younger,* Rachel thought. Ellen looked even more frail. She was thin and pale and looked as if something had happened to her face. Her nose was flat and misshapen as if it had been broken, but her eyes were bright, and she seemed very kind and friendly. Rachel decided she liked her.

"My papa is a reporter for a newspaper," Rachel explained, "and he's been covering a lot of the religion stories in the news the past few years."

James nodded. "Yes, there have been many of them," he agreed.

"Yes," Rachel said, "and Papa thinks they're all a bunch of religious nuts."

Papa nudged Rachel again. "Oh," she said, "I'm so sorry. That probably sounded really rude." James and Ellen burst out laughing.

"Yes," Ellen agreed. "There are a lot of religious nuts out there, and there are some people who really, really love God. Sometimes it's hard to tell the difference between the two."

Rachel nodded.

"James and I have been to visit some who were pretty confused. They believed that they were perfect now and could not sin, so anything they did obviously wasn't a sin. And others believe they must become like little children to enter the kingdom of heaven, so they crawl around on the floor and act like babies."

Rachel wrinkled her nose. "Do you think it's right for people to do things that are so weird that they make God look foolish? I love

143

God, and I want people to respect Him and think He's wonderful and a King, not think that following Him makes you stupid."

Papa smiled, still a little uncomfortable.

"Well," Ellen said, "there have been times when God has asked people to do things that seemed a little strange. If God asks you to do something, you should do it no matter what it is, but I believe that following God makes good logical sense. If we use the Bible to check out everything we are told, we'll always be safe."

"Really? The Bible backs up everything?"

"Oh yes," Ellen assured her. "That's what we've been talking to Captain Bates about this week—this Sabbath thing."

"It's in the Bible too?" Rachel queried.

"Of course." Papa spoke for the first time in several minutes. "The Jews kept the Sabbath, and it's in the Jewish law in the Old Testament."

"But we are not Jews," Rachel pointed out.

"That's true," James admitted. "And Ellen and I have been talking about this a lot. Captain Bates believes that God never changed that law, and he has done some historical research on it. Apparently it was changed by people hundreds of years after Jesus lived here on earth. And it was changed for convenience."

"Well, if that's true," Rachel observed, "then we should probably still be keeping the day that God asked us to keep in the first place."

"Exactly," Mrs. Bates agreed. "That's what my husband says."

James and Ellen looked uncomfortable. "We aren't sure about this yet," they said, "but that's what we came here to talk about."

"Well, good," Rachel said. "My papa came here to see Captain Bates and to learn more about this too, because he's writing a story for the newspaper about it. So we can all talk about it together."

CAPTAIN JOSEPH BATES'S HOME, FAIR HAVEN, MASSACHUSETTS: FALL 1846

Rachel continued to sip her lemonade as she glanced around the parlor. "You have a beautiful parlor, Mrs. Bates," she said.

"Why, thank you," said Mrs. Bates.

"We have a nice parlor too," said Rachel, "but we aren't rich like you and the captain." Mrs. Bates colored slightly, and Papa nudged Rachel again.

"Actually," said Mrs. Bates, "we *were* rich. When Joseph retired from the sea, we had a nice nest egg put away, and we were planning to live very comfortably, but we spent it all helping the Advent movement. We wanted everyone to know Jesus was coming."

"But He didn't come," Rachel added.

"I know," Mrs. Bates said. "And since then Joseph has spent it helping to support the Advent groups who are still expecting Jesus to come, or on this Sabbath thing. In fact, a couple weeks ago we had quite a to-do here. Joseph had decided to write a little book about the Sabbath. We were just about out of money. He hadn't told me yet, but here he was, busily working away on a book that he had no funds to publish and no idea where money was coming from. I was baking in the kitchen and ran out of flour, so I asked him to go to the store and get me some."

"'How much do you need?' he asked me. 'Oh, about four pounds,' I said. He about shocked my bonnet off when he came back with only four pounds of flour. I didn't even know you could buy only four pounds of flour. I thought it came in hundred-pound barrels. Then Joseph explained to me that he bought only four pounds of flour because that's all the money he had. I was quite upset."

"I can imagine," Rachel sympathized, "after being so rich."

Papa nudged Rachel in the ribs again.

"Oh, sorry."

"Yes," Mrs. Bates continued, "that's exactly what I was thinking. I burst into tears and was very angry at Joseph. But God has taken such good care of us. Joseph stood up and said he thought there was a letter for him at the post office, and off he went. I have no idea where he gets these impressions from, but sure enough, there was a letter at the post office. Unfortunately, whoever sent it hadn't put enough postage on it, and he owed five cents."

"But he didn't have five cents," Rachel insisted.

"That's right," said Mrs. Bates. "He asked the postmaster to go ahead and open the letter and if there was money in it, he could take out five cents from it. If not, Joseph said he wouldn't read it. The postmaster opened the letter, and there was a ten-dollar bill in it. So Joseph ended up paying the postage and buying groceries for us, and more than five pounds of flour. I was still crying and angry with Joseph when the delivery man came and piled all this stuff on the porch. I'm afraid I yelled at him too. I told him that we had no money and that he needed to take it back to the store and get it off my porch."

Everyone laughed.

"Of course he ignored me. Then Joseph explained what had happened. God is good to us."

"God is good," Rachel repeated. "And I'm sure He will continue to take care of you. After all, you spent all your money for Him."

Everyone nodded. Yes, God is faithful to those who are faithful to Him.

＊ ＊ ＊

"And so," Rachel told Uriah, "God sent ten dollars to Captain Bates and took care of his groceries, leaving him enough so that he could put out his little book about the Sabbath."

"Wow," Uriah said. "Mrs. Bates must have felt embarrassed for having been so angry at him and forgetting that God would take care of them."

"Yes, I guess," Rachel answered, "but sometimes I forget too."

Uriah nodded. "Yes, I've gotten pretty discouraged a few times." Both of their minds drifted back to that terrible day in October 1844, but neither of them mentioned it.

"And you know what else?" Rachel asked. "Captain Bates doesn't smoke, doesn't drink, and eats only vegetarian food—no meat, no grease, no butter, and no spices."

"What does he eat?" asked Uriah. "That doesn't leave much."

"I know," said Rachel. "When we were there for lunch, though, we had fruit and lots of vegetables with bread, and it was really all right. Papa asked him why he didn't eat any of those things, and he just said, 'Oh, I've had my share,' but Mrs. Bates told us later that he does it for his health. He doesn't try to make other people do what he does. He just quietly does it until we all ask questions about it."

"He's really smart," Uriah observed. "Most people hate to be told what to do, but we're all pretty curious creatures."

"That's true," Rachel agreed, "but the most interesting thing was the visitors who were there. James and Ellen White were visiting. They were Millerites like us, only they have stayed in the little Advent group. Ellen White told us all about a vision that she had soon after the Great Disappointment. She dreamed that she was looking for the Advent people, but she couldn't find them. A voice told her to look a little higher, and when she did, she saw a narrow path up above the world. It was going to heaven, and we were all traveling on it."

"We were?" Uriah asked.

"Well, the Advent people anyway," Rachel said. "But that would be us. We were looking for Jesus to come."

"We were," Uriah agreed.

"Well, anyway," Rachel continued, "there was a light up at the beginning that lit the path so the travelers wouldn't stumble, and an angel told her it was the Midnight Cry. In front of the company, leading them, was Jesus, and as long as His followers kept their eyes fixed on Him, they were safe, but when they got tired and complained and looked away, they stumbled and fell off the path."

"We do need to keep our eyes on Jesus," Uriah said. "When we don't is usually when we run into trouble."

"She said," Rachel told him, "that some grew tired and complained that the city was too far away. Jesus raised His arm, and a light shone from it all along the path. Most of the people shouted with joy, but some lost sight of Him and said they weren't sure it had been God who had led them at all. For them the light went out; they were left in complete darkness, and they fell off the path too."

"H'mm," Uriah said. "It sounds like the Millerites."

"Yes," Rachel replied, "it does. She also told us she heard the voice of God telling the group the day and the hour of Jesus' coming. When they saw Him come, they got worried and cried, 'Who shall be able to stand?' There was a terrible silence."

"I know how they must feel," Uriah said slowly. "Sometimes I don't feel ready to meet Jesus either. I try really hard to be good."

"Well, the voice of Jesus spoke in her vision and said, 'Those who have clean hands and pure hearts shall be able to stand; My grace is sufficient for you.' Everyone was delighted, and the angels sang. She saw dead people coming out of their graves and getting together with their loved ones. They were very happy and they all went to heaven with Jesus. He told them, 'You who have washed your robes in my blood and stood stiffly for my truth, enter in.' And she got to enter the city in heaven. Doesn't that sound wonderful?"

"It does," Uriah said, "it really does. What an encouragement!"

"Oh, there's more," Rachel said. "Joseph Bates told us all about the Sabbath, and I've decided to start keeping it."

"Really?" said Uriah. "This vision stuff sounds encouraging, but it's kind of weird. I heard Mrs. White got hit on the head really hard when she was younger and is kind of brain-damaged."

Rachel explained. "Her face is kind of odd and scarred, but I thought she was pretty smart and intelligent. She didn't seem brain-damaged to me."

I watched as Rachel opened her Bible and showed Uriah the texts that Captain Bates had shared with her during her visit.

Uriah listened to it all patiently and then said, "I don't know, Rachel. A lot of it makes sense, but I just don't feel comfortable with these visions. I guess I'll have to think about it some more."

"Well," Rachel answered, "I'll have to think about it some more too. I'm not sure of a lot of things, but this thing I am sure of. I really love God, and if He asked us to keep the Sabbath and never asked us not to, then I want to make Him happy by still keeping it. It seems to me that we must have misunderstood something about the day Jesus was coming, and I really think He sent Ellen to encourage us. Maybe someday He'll even explain the rest of it, and we'll understand it all."

"Maybe so," Uriah said. "But it's just hard for me to accept my theology from a girl who is the same age as Annie."

Rachel looked down at the floor. "Well, that's true," she said. "She is only six months older than Annie, but God didn't always use important church people in the Bible when He wanted to teach people things. Sometimes He used shepherds and farmers and even kids younger than Annie. Maybe even kids younger than me."

"Well, I'll think about it," Uriah promised.

I smiled as I watched the two study and discuss. I knew that the Almighty would give guidance to anyone open to thinking about it, and that they would find the truth eventually.

OSWEGO, NEW YORK: FALL 1849

"I'm glad I got to come with you again, Papa," Rachel said. "It's been a long time since our last trip."

"Yes," Papa said, laughing. "You are 15 now, and let's hope you have learned a few more manners and are a little more tactful than that time I took you to see the Bates family."

Rachel laughed. "I'm sorry I embarrassed you," she said. "It's just that everything was so interesting, and I had so many questions."

"I know," Papa said, "and I've always been proud of you even when you're a little tactless."

"Well, I will be the absolute epitome of tactfulness and good manners this time," Rachel promised. "You can count on me."

"Well, good," Papa replied. "I am counting on you, and I'm glad that your mama agreed to let you come with me. You're growing up so fast. Pretty soon you're going to be leaving home and won't be able to go places with me anymore. We'll look back and remember these good times together."

Rachel smiled. "I'm really excited about seeing Elder and Mrs. White again. I've seen them a few times when they've come through Washington on their trips to visit the other Sabbath-keepers. I don't know if they'll remember me or not, but I sure remember them."

"Well, I imagine they haven't forgotten you," Papa said.

"Well," Rachel predicted, "they may not have forgotten you. Not all of the stories that you've put in the paper have been particularly complimentary."

"Well," said Papa, "newspapers have to be objective. They can't get caught up in all this religious stuff."

Rachel looked at her shoes. I knew that she prayed for her papa every night, and I knew that the Almighty had sent His Spirit to work on his heart. It's a pretty powerful force to resist, although the Mighty One has always allowed humans to have a free choice in this matter.

"So, Papa, tell me what's happening on this trip. What are you going to check out?"

"Well," Papa said, "at the paper we heard that there's a little trouble here in Oswego. You know that James and Ellen White have moved here to start their little publishing venture."

"Yes," Rachel agreed. "Their first paper came out in July. It's called *The Present Truth.*"

"Yes, I know," Papa continued. "I saw it too, but some of the other church people here in Oswego are unhappy with the things they are teaching, particularly their Sabbath message. These people are going to hold a religious revival and are trying to convince the people that the Sabbath is not important as long as they turn away from their sins and give their hearts to God."

"Oh," Rachel said. "Well, turning away from your sins and giving your heart to God is important. That would be the first step, but once you give your heart to God, you love Him that much, you want to please Him. He told us 'If you love me, you'll keep My commandments.' He said that in the Bible, in John."

"Yes, I know," Papa said. "I'm just telling you what's going on here in Oswego and what I'm coming to report on. The religious revival has been going on for about a month, and right now it looks like town opinion is swaying toward the Methodist leaders. However, we're going to be staying with a friend of mine named Mr. Patch. He hasn't made up his mind yet, and he told me a most interesting story."

"You talked to Mr. Patch already?" asked Rachel.

"No," said Papa. "He wrote me a letter. He and I are friends from way back. Apparently Ellen White told Mr. Patch, 'Just wait for a month, and you will be shown the character of the people engaged in this revival who profess to have such a great burden for sinners.' Mr. Patch knows who the leader is and whom she was talking about. He says that Mrs. White was given a vision, and she knows something that she's not going to tell, but he will find out. It's been about a month, and I thought we would come and visit Mr. Patch and see if we could learn what this big secret is."

"Sounds like it would make a good story," Rachel said, "if there's anything we can actually find out, or if Mrs. White decides to tell."

* * *

Mr. Patch was delighted to see them. "I'm so glad you brought Rachel," he said. And turning to her he added, "I haven't seen you since you were a little tyke."

Rachel wrinkled her nose. She hated to be told how much she had grown.

"Well, come on in and have a seat—get comfortable," he invited them. "I'll have your bags brought in in a few minutes. Do you have any questions you want to ask? I know you're full of them."

"Sure," Papa said. "Um, how are James and Ellen White viewed in town here?"

"I guess it depends who's viewing them," Mr. Patch replied. "James seems to be pretty well respected. Apparently last fall he was still trying to raise money for food and supplies for their publishing venture. He took a job in the harvest field cutting grain."

"James White cutting grain?" Papa queried.

"He looks a little, well, feeble for that?" Mr. Patch asked.

"Well, I was looking for a kinder word than that," Papa said, "but yes."

"It's true," Mr. Patch continued. "He has not always been in good health, and apparently he had an ankle injury working in a sawmill when he was younger that crippled his left foot for years."

"Yes," Papa said. "He still has a bit of a limp."

"Well, the other farmhands don't have much use for preachers and such, and they weren't real excited about his doing the harvesting with them. James himself wasn't sure he could do that type of hard field work. They decided to put him at the head of the grain-cutting team."

"What would that do?" Rachel asked.

"Well, they follow each other in a diagonal line. Each one cuts a swath, and the next one behind him cuts his swath where the first man's strip began and goes across. The man at the head has the hardest job. He has to keep ahead of all the others and set the pace. They were hoping to run him down and drive him off the field."

"How mean!" Rachel exclaimed.

"Yes, I suppose," Mr. Patch said. "But these are tough men. Anyway, apparently James cut a very wide swath and kept swinging his scythe just as fast as he could. The other men were taking narrower ones so they could go faster and keep as close to him as possible, hoping to run over him. Across the wide field they worked and worked. Then they turned around and started back with James still ahead of them. Finally the men threw down their scythes. They were furious. 'You're trying to kill yourself and us too,' they shouted. 'We give up! We can't even keep up with you. And you did all that without even a beer?'"

Rachel laughed. "James doesn't drink beer."

"Apparently not," Mr. Patch said. "When he walked onto that field, they were angry and determined to give him a hard time. Now he has the respect of the farmers and the hardworking men. However, the church people aren't as excited about him, and many people don't know what to make of his wife, who has these visions."

"Right," Rachel agreed. "She told you about a vision, didn't she?"

"Yes," Mr. Patch said. "She says I'm going to find out something about the leadership of this revival."

"Well, we'll go with you to the meeting," Rachel stated, "because we want to find out too."

"All right," Mr. Patch said. "I don't really know what to think on this. I'm torn between the two. After her accident when she was nine years old, she was so ill and disabled that she wasn't even able to complete her education past third grade. I understand that she has had headaches, eye inflammation, respiratory weaknesses, and even perhaps tuberculosis. The doctors said that she had no hope and was going to experience an early death. She has heart trouble too, and in December of 1844, when she had that first vision, she was wheelchair bound at the Haines' house. She couldn't even speak above a whisper."

"Wow!" Rachel exclaimed. "I didn't realize she was so sick."

"Yes," Mr. Patch continued. "And she still is ill off and on. Yet no matter how ill she is, when she stands up to speak, she speaks in a clear voice, for up to four hours at a time once, without looking tired. Even if she's pale as a ghost when she stands up, the color comes back into her face, and she seems to get her strength back. It's an amazing transformation from weakness to power. It has happened many times."

"It sounds quite convincing," Papa said.

"Well, it is, and when she has her visions sometimes she doesn't even breathe—she doesn't move—and strong men can't move her arms from the position she's in. It's just amazing, yet I'm still torn. I just don't know. I've been Methodist all my life, and I have a lot of respect for the men leading the revival right now. I don't know what to think."

"Well," Papa said, "we'll stay a few days and talk to a few people, and we'll even go to the meetings with you. What time is the meeting time tonight? Is there time for us to rest a little first and change our clothes?"

"Oh, sure," Mr. Patch answered. "Let me show you your rooms."

That night Rachel and her father attended the revival meetings with Mr. Patch and his fiancée. Mr. Mitchell (not his real name), the county treasurer, was one of the leaders at the revival. After the sermon he prayed loud and long, agonizing over the sinners in the congregation. Suddenly, in the middle of the prayer, he grabbed his stomach and doubled up in terrible pain.

"What's the matter?" Rachel whispered.

"I don't know," Mr. Patch said. "Let's get him some help."

Mr. Patch rushed to the front, and with several other men carried Mr. Mitchell home. On the way Mr. Mitchell started vomiting blood.

* * *

"Well, nothing has happened," Papa remarked at breakfast a few days later. "I think I need to get back to Washington."

"Well," Mr. Patch said, "we did have the excitement over Mr. Mitchell."

"Yes," Papa admitted, "but that hardly constitutes an evil character being exposed. That's not the same thing as a broken blood vessel in a man's stomach, even if it was quite dramatic."

"True," Mr. Patch agreed. "You may want to wait one more day, though. I heard that those trying to do Mr. Mitchell's work at the courthouse have found that a thousand dollars is missing from county funds."

"Really?" Papa's ears perked up. "That sounds like a news story."

"The sheriff and his assistant are going over there this morning, but no one's supposed to know yet."

"I think I'll follow them," Papa said. He rushed out to go chat with the sheriff.

Half an hour later the sheriff went to the front door of the sick man's home and knocked. Papa and the sheriff's assistant stayed out in the yard. Suddenly Papa noticed a movement on the other side of the house.

"Let's go check it out," he whispered to the assistant.

One went around each side of the house. Mrs. Mitchell was sneaking out the back door carrying a bag. She rushed over to a snowbank and dug a hole, dropping the bag quickly into the pile and pushing snow over it. The sheriff's assistant grabbed her by the wrist and made her go back with him as he pulled the bag out of the snowbank. Then he and Papa went inside.

They came into Mr. Mitchell's bedroom just in time to hear him saying, "I swear as God as my witness, I didn't take any money from the county."

The assistant held up the bag and asked, "Then what is this?" Sure enough, it contained the missing money.

* * *

"Well," Mr. Patch said. "Aren't you glad you waited another day? Now you have the whole story."

"I guess I do," Papa said. "This is just amazing. How did Ellen White know?"

"I don't know," Mr. Patch said. "I think the Lord really does talk to her. At any rate, nobody thinks the Lord talks to Mr. Mitchell."

"I feel sad for Mr. Mitchell," Rachel remarked. "It must be awful to be recovering from a bleeding stomach and be put in jail too."

"Yes," Mr. Patch agreed, "I imagine it is. But this whole thing has helped me make up my mind. I'm going to join the Sabbathkeeping Advent group. How about you?"

"Well, Rachel already is one," Papa admitted, "and . . . I think I'm going to have to join too." Rachel jumped up in delight and hugged her papa.

"Papa, I'm so glad," she whispered. "I've been praying about this for a long time."

"I know," said Papa, grinning. "I just can't hold out any longer."

EPILOGUE

The little band of Sabbathkeepers grew rapidly into what is now known as the Seventh-day Adventist Church.

Uriah invented a jointed prosthetic leg instead of the usual wooden peg legs available to amputees at that time. He became an Adventist, and so did his sister, Annie. Both were poets and prolific writers. Uriah became editor of The Review and Herald, *and Annie wrote many of the early Adventist hymns still enjoyed today.*

The Almighty continued to give messages through Ellen, while her husband, James, was gifted with organizational skills and served as the second president of the General Conference after the Seventh-day Adventists had formed their church organization in 1863.

Through this group and others, such as the Seventh Day Baptists, the Sabbath message was spread all over the world. Other Millerites who accepted the Sabbath formed the Advent Christian Church.

William Miller died in 1849, still waiting for Jesus to come. He never accepted the Sabbath.

Michael

FOSTER HOME: A.D. 2???

ike lay on his bed and buried his face in his pillow. He had never felt more miserable. Life all seemed to fall apart when his mom died. She had been sick for a long time, but he never thought she would actually die. Several times she had been close to death, but they had always prayed hard and called the elders to anoint her, just as the Bible says, and she usually got better. This time she didn't.

Meanwhile, all the floods, hurricanes, and earthquakes in the United States had caused the government to change several laws, because the entire country was in a state of disaster. Yet Mike hardly noticed it. Those first few months were a blur.

If anything good had come from the disasters, it was that the country was turning back to God. But even though Mike and his family believed in God, they just didn't fit in. Everyone seemed to be setting aside their differences, and anyone who wouldn't was considered uncooperative. In no time Dad was viewed as one of those renegades and lumped together with the antigovernment, nontax-paying militia-type of people hiding in the mountains. His social security number was entered into the federal computers, and he wasn't allowed to buy or sell anything. He also got fired from his job.

Mike rolled over and stared at the peeling wallpaper in the bedroom of his foster home. It hadn't been long before some folks had come from Social Services. They had said that Dad couldn't keep him, since he couldn't even pay his bills. They had called him a deadbeat, and police officers had been there in case there was any trouble. Mike had stared out the back window of the car, watching Dad standing on the hill in front of his house. How could God have let this happen?

He hadn't heard from anybody since. Mike was sure Dad would have written to him, so the authorities must not have been letting the letters through. Mrs. Beasley said that Dad was in jail, that he was a criminal, and that's where he belonged. She said he had done a lot of bad things. If Dad was in jail, where was Don?

"Hey, man, are you OK?" a voice asked.

Mike rolled over and looked up.

"My name's Pete. I guess I'm your roommate."

Mike nodded and closed his eyes again.

"You think they're hard of hearing down there?" Pete asked. "TV's on so loud you can hear it up here even with the door closed."

Mike nodded. "Yeah," he said, "stone deaf unless you say something they don't like. Then they hear really well."

That was it for conversation. Both boys lay on their beds listening to the TV in the background: "There's been an outbreak of a new virus. Seventy-three people are infected in Atlanta; strains of the virus have been discovered also in Seattle, New York, and London. The Center for Disease Control is scrambling to find the method of transmission. It seems to be spreading fast. More news at 10 o'clock."

Mike rolled over. "I don't know why they even listen to

that," he said. "The only thing more depressing than our lives is the news."

Pete nodded. "Yup," he said. "Wars, floods, famines, and disasters. Pretty apocalyptic, don't you think?"

Mike grinned. "Since I was a little boy, whenever anything happened, people always said it was a sign of the times, or that it read like Matthew 24. But somehow this isn't like I imagined the time of trouble to be. Maybe it's just my own private time of trouble."

"I don't know," Pete said. "It sounds like people are being massacred all over the planet."

"Yeah," Mike agreed. He turned toward the wall with his back to Pete. He didn't want to talk about it. Nobody could understand the misery he was going through. He wished his brother, Don, could be here. He and his brother had always been very close. Don was 18, so he counted as an adult. Would he be able to get a job? Would he be able to find food? How come he hadn't written?

STATE PENITENTIARY: A.D. 2???

Bruce hit the wall and slumped to the floor in the little gray cell. "If you can't get along with people, you're going to have to do some time by yourself," said the guard, slamming the door shut.

Bruce tried to get up on his hands and knees, but he slumped to the floor. His face felt wet and sticky, and he had never hurt so badly all over. The last hour had gone by in a painful blur. "So you like beatin' up little kids, do ya?" one of the inmates snarled. "Hey, maybe you'd like a taste of your own medicine. How d'ya like that?"

"But I didn't," Bruce said. "I never beat up anyone." But he never got a chance to explain any further.

"Hey, I hear your wife is dead. Did you beat her up too?"

"Yeah, how do you like it?" another asked.

"O Lord, please help me," Bruce whispered, and he felt a crushing blow to his head. After that he seemed kind of numb. He was aware of the kicking and the punching, but it was as if he were watching it from across the room. "Please God, just take care of my boys," he groaned as he lost consciousness.

The last thing he knew he was being dumped in solitary confinement. As he spit the blood from his mouth, he realized he was missing a few teeth. He smiled through cracked and bleeding lips. "Thanks for solitary confinement, God," he said. "At least nobody is going to beat on me here. Please take care of my boys too, and especially be close to Mike. He's too young to be alone right now. And please help Don, wherever he is. I know he's 18, but he still seems like a little boy to me."

Suddenly all his pain seemed far away, and everything faded to darkness.

MIDDLE EAST DESERT ARMY CAMP: A.D. 2???

"Yes, sir, I'll carry this gun if you want me to," Don said, "but with all due respect, sir, I can't shoot those guys."

"Of course you can," his sergeant barked.

Don looked him coolly in the eye. "I'm a medic, sir," he said. "My job is to put people back together. I'm not killing anyone, sir."

"You'll do what you're ordered," the sergeant shouted.

Don stood in silence.

"Can you tell me why in heaven's name you don't want to shoot these Arab towel-heads when you know that if you don't shoot them, they're gonna shoot you?"

"That might be, sir," Don answered, "but I don't kill people."

Mom and Dad had sent him to a school that was a real racial melting pot. Kids from China, Jamaica, the Philippines, Brazil, Vietnam, and Hungary were there. He had learned that everyone has external differences, but underneath, kids have the same feelings and fears. He just couldn't bring himself to shoot at a bunch of kids who happened to be the enemy, but who probably had as little choice about being at war as he did.

"Then what on earth are you doing in the army?" the sergeant shouted.

"I had no choice, sir," replied Don evenly, "but I'm willing to take care of you or anyone else who gets wounded. I'm willing to work as hard as the others. I just can't kill people."

"You'll do what you're ordered, or you'll spend the rest of this war and the rest of your life in the brig. We'll throw away the key, and you can rot, as far as I'm concerned," the sergeant bellowed, turning purple. "To your quarters, before I shoot you myself!"

"Yes, sir," Don answered and turned to walk away.

"Lock him up," the sergeant ordered. Two other soldiers grabbed Don by the arms and dragged him away.

"You don't have to do that," said Don. "I'll come with you."

The two soldiers looked at the ground. As soon as they were around the corner and out of the sergeant's view they let go. Don stood up.

"Come on," they said. "We have to do this."

"I know," Don said.

He followed them to the brig. Leaning against the concrete wall in the silence of his cell, he remembered how badly Mike had wanted to be a soldier when he was a little guy. He also remembered how much it bothered Mom and how many times she had said to him, "Mike, I've spent my whole career putting people's bodies back together again. I just can't stand the idea of one of my kids blowing them apart for a living." Don sighed. If Mom were around now, at least she'd be pleased with his decision.

He closed his eyes. "God, what are You doing?" he asked. "The whole world is going to Hades in a handbasket, and everything that possibly can go wrong is going wrong. I couldn't get a job, so the only choice I had was to join the military or go to jail like Dad. Hmph! Big difference it made! God, please take care of my dad wherever he is. Don't let them hurt him."

Don shuddered as he thought of all the things the newspaper said his dad had done. He knew that people in jail could be pretty tough on child abusers. Would the people in jail know he was innocent? Wasn't that what they all say? Well, at least Mike is in a safe place. "God, please be close to him. I wish I knew where he is."

Don had called Social Services again and again, but no one would give him any information.

"If you're not the child's parent, I really can't help you," the lady would say. "Please don't call this number again, or we'll have to report it."

Now I'll never find him, Don thought. "But God, You know where he is. Please take care of him."

I smiled as I watched the three men all praying for each other at the same time. Within seconds extra guardians were assigned to all three. They would need them.

* * *

"Mike, why don't you come on downstairs and watch cartoons with the other guys?" Mrs. Beasley invited.

"I don't feel like it," Mike answered.

"Well, you can't just lie around up here. I know you're depressed, but you need to become part of the group."

"I'd rather stay in here," Mike said. "I don't want to watch television right now."

Mrs. Beasley frowned. "You don't mind watching television, Mike," she said pointedly. "You just don't want to come down because it's your Sabbath, and you think watching TV now is wrong."

Mike met her gaze but said nothing.

"Well, what makes you think you're so much better than everyone else? Get yourself downstairs right now."

Mike stood. "I guess I have to do whatever you tell me to," he said. "But you can't keep me from keeping Sabbath in my heart, no matter where you make me go or what's going on in the room."

"Listen, Mike," Mrs. Beasley said, taking on a softer tone. "You come from a good Christian home. Didn't your parents ever teach you about grace?"

"Of course," Mike answered. "I wouldn't be a Christian if I didn't believe in grace."

"Well, you're obviously still trying to earn your own salvation by works."

"What do you mean?" Mike asked.

"Well, when Jesus died on the cross, His blood covered everything. You don't have to keep the old Jewish Sabbath anymore. You don't have to earn your salvation by keeping the Ten Commandments. We're under grace now."

"Ah," Mike said. "I see what you're getting at."

"Good," said Mrs. Beasley, breaking into a smile.

"But I'm not earning it. There's not a thing I could do to deserve salvation, and I know that. I'm just glad that God did save me, and the best way for me to show Him I love Him is to keep His commandments. All of them."

"I'm going to make an appointment with the psychiatrist for you, Mike," she said. "You're just obsessed with these stupid religious ideas. I've tried really hard to be kind and to help you, but it's obviously going to take something else." She walked out and slammed the door.

Pete opened his eyes and grinned at Mike. "She sounds pretty mad," he observed.

Mike grinned back, "Can't please everyone," he said. "I picked one Person, and it's not her."

Pete laughed. "You picked God."

"Yeah," Mike replied. "It sounds kind of funny to say it out loud, but it's what I'm doing."

"Well," Pete reasoned, "if you can please only one person per day, I guess God is a good choice."

"Yeah," Mike said, "today isn't Mrs. Beasley's day, and tomorrow doesn't look good for her either."

Pete chuckled. "Good for you."

I chuckled too. Even in this horrible time period, there were some bright spots.

SOLITARY CONFINEMENT, STATE PENITENTIARY: A.D. 2???

When Bruce woke up, it was dark. He figured it must be nighttime, since the guards had turned out the light in his cell, but he could still see a crack of light in the door where the sliding panel was. The guards watched him through it. It was big enough to slide a plate through. Maybe they would feed him through it too.

He crawled over to the cot fastened to the wall and rolled onto it. It was better than the floor. He closed his eyes. "God, I feel so alone. I feel as if I must have messed up somehow and let You down. After all, Your followers pay their bills, and whether or not I did those things they are accusing me of, it can't be a very good witness for everyone in the world to think I did." He sighed. "Are You watching? Do You remember I'm here?"

The darkness seemed almost to suffocate him. The tears brimming in his eyes spilled over now and stung the cuts on his cheek. In the background someone was whistling. At first he didn't notice it, but it continued on and on. He rolled over on his side and propped up on his elbow to listen. It was the same song over and over. He smiled. It reminded him of when his wife was sick. She would get her favorite tapes and listen to them over and over again until it drove everyone nuts. Mike finally lent her his Walkman so that she would use headphones.

The song was a familiar one, and as the whistling continued, he puckered his bruised lips and whistled a little. At first he just made a hissing sound through his cracked teeth, but he was persistent, and soon he was whistling. A feeling of peace came over him, and once again he fell asleep.

MIDDLE EAST DESERT CAMP, MILITARY BRIG: a.D. 2???

Don was shaken awake by explosions all around him. The window grate in his cell was too high for him to see what was happening outside, but it was obviously an attack of some kind. He could hear the rockets and missiles whistling overhead and crashing into the buildings and grounds around him. The flashes illuminated his entire cell.

He lay on the floor and rolled under his bunk for a moment, then thought better of it and rolled back out again. He knelt instead. *If I am going to take a direct hit,* he thought, *I'd rather be on my knees anyway.* "God," he prayed out loud, "I guess it doesn't matter whether I get shot by somebody for refusing to shoot the enemy or whether I get bombed in this prison. I belong to You. You can take care of me. You can pick up the pieces and create me all new when this is over." Before he had a chance to continue, a brilliant flash of light dazzled him. He was thrown across the small cell into the inside wall.

He let his mind wander, imagining that suddenly in the midst of it all he would look up and see Jesus coming. Choking and gagging on the dust, he opened his eyes and realized that the outside wall was gone! All around him were flashes of light and the chatter of gunfire. He slowly crawled to the open wall. Not far away was an outcropping of rocks. If he could just get to that, it would give him some shelter as he decided what to do next. He looked both ways and then headed for the rocks.

Once safely behind the rocks, he surveyed the situation. The camp was a chaotic bombed-out mess, with buildings and vehicles burning and filling the air with black smoke.

A narrow rocky gully led up the hillside, and Don ran for that. Rounding an outcropping of rocks, he stumbled onto two men lying on the ground. One was bleeding profusely. Don paused. Should he stop to help or keep running? A huge explosion sprung him forward, but then he stopped. God hadn't delivered him from the brig to leave a wounded person when helping wounded people was the whole reason he was there anyway. He turned and looked closely at the first man. He had a dark complexion, but Don couldn't tell if he was an ally or an enemy. He was not in a uniform—just the voluminous robes worn in the desert by those who lived there.

"Uh, hi," Don greeted them. "Either of you speak English?" No response.

Don held his hands out. "See, I don't have a weapon," he said slowly. "You look as if you are hurt."

Don knelt, ripped off part of the man's robe, and used it to staunch the bleeding and to make a bandage for his leg. The bleeding stopped; he turned to the other man. He was in obvious pain, and his left arm was at an odd angle. Don made a makeshift splint for his arm and gently checked him over. Apart from a large lump on the back of his head, he seemed OK.

Suddenly three more men dashed out from behind the rocks. Two of them grabbed the man with the broken arm and helped him to his feet, then picked up the other injured man and carried him behind the rocks. The third man grabbed Don's arm and motioned him to follow.

A sudden explosion even closer than the last helped him over any indecision he may have felt, and he followed the men around the rocks. They crawled into a small opening, dragging their wounded with them. The last man motioned for Don to crawl in ahead of him.

After crawling for what seemed like forever, the passage opened into a large chamber. When Don entered, several more people jumped to their feet, staring at him in astonishment. The man who led him into the cave began to speak rapidly in a language Don did not understand.

Arabic? he wondered. *Probably.*

Soon the man who had motioned him into the cave brought him a bowl of lentils and some flat bread. Don nodded thankfully and ate. *They may not speak English,* he thought, *but they don't seem to plan to kill me, and I feel a lot safer in here than in the brig!*

A smoky fire curled up toward a crack in the ceiling. Don moved closer to the fire. "Thank You, God!" he whispered. "I think I've found some friends. Perhaps I'll be safe here for a while." He curled up and within minutes fell into the soundest sleep he had experienced in weeks.

* * *

"Mike, we're only trying to help you," the psychiatrist said. "Now I want you to close your eyes and just allow your mind to empty."

Mike grinned. "I've never had an empty mind in my life," he joked. "I have a very busy brain."

"You're not cooperating, Mike," she snapped. "I want you to be at absolute rest so that you can go within yourself and find your spirit guide."

"My Spirit Guide isn't within myself," Mike said. "I don't have anybody else in here but me. My Spirit Guide is outside myself. Remember God?"

"Within yourself or outside yourself—what does it matter?" the psychiatrist snapped. "Lie back and close your eyes. I'm trying to teach you some self-hypnosis to help you deal with your problems."

"Well, I don't believe in hypnosis," Mike said, "and I don't believe in letting anyone else control my mind, either. Besides, my mind is the only thing I still have any control over. You can't take that away from me."

"You are a stubborn kid," interjected Mrs. Beasley, who had been sitting in on the session.

"Yeah, that's what my mom always used to say too."

"Were you close to your mother?" the doctor asked.

Mike nodded and looked at the floor.

Maybe this is a better tack to take, the counselor thought. "What kind of advice do you think your mom would give now?"

Mike continued to look at the floor. He remembered sitting on her lap asking a thousand questions. She always took time to answer. His favorite one was "Why?" Ever since he'd been 2 years old, he had asked, "Why?" and his questions became more complex as he grew. He remembered Mom explaining hypnosis to him—how it worked, what it was, and how God never intended for anyone else to control his mind.

He raised his eyes. "I'll tell you what my mom would say . . ."

But as he began to explain, the counselor cut him off. "We can help you with that," she said. "We can put you in touch with her."

"What about my dad instead?" Mike asked hopefully. "My mom died a year ago. Remember?"

The counselor shook her head. "Your dad is not a particularly good influence. As I recall, he is incarcerated right now, but we can help you get in touch with the other side. You can still get guidance from your mom."

Mike frowned.

"Close your eyes and relax," the psychiatrist ordered. "Look! Here she is now."

Mike spun around. Mom was sitting in the other chair in the office.

"Mikey," she said. "I've missed you so much."

Mike felt the tears burn behind his eyes. He wanted to say "I've missed you too." He wanted to throw himself in her lap and beg her to take him away, but he sat rigidly in his chair.

"Who are you?" he asked.

"Mike, don't you remember me? It hasn't been that long." Her eyes filled with tears.

"How could you hurt your mom's feelings like that?" demanded Mrs. Beasley.

Mike's feelings were all messed up. He felt happy and excited and sad and angry all at once, and everything was pounding through his veins in a coarse, confused jumble.

"You look like my mom," he said, "but you're not. People can't raise the dead. They can only impersonate them. You know who you are, and I know who you are."

A look of anger flashed across her face. She leaped to her feet and lunged toward Mike, and then she was gone.

"Look what you did!" Mrs. Beasley snapped.

"This is just not working out." The psychiatrist looked annoyed. "Mike, your lack of cooperation is making it impossible for us to help you. We'll set another appointment for next week, and in the meantime you need an attitude adjustment, young man. I want you to think about this."

Back in his room that night, Mike told Pete what had happened.

"But that's right," Pete said. "It wasn't your mom. I know you really miss her, but that wasn't her. The way things are going, I think you'll get to see your real mom again—and soon."

"You think so?" Mike asked hopefully.

"Yeah, I do. God hasn't forgotten us. He's coming back for us very soon, and when He does, you'll be back together with your family again. It's going to be OK, Mike."

Mike flipped out the light and buried his face in his pillow. It was uncool to cry in front of your roommate. "O God," he whispered after he got back in control, "please come soon. I really need You."

SOLITARY CONFINEMENT, STATE PENITENTIARY: a.D. 2???

With a clang, the slot in the door slid open. "Hey, time to wake up if you want some breakfast," the guard yelled.

"Thanks," Bruce said, taking the plate as slowly as possible. Here was another human being. He had gotten quite lonely in the solitary cell over the past few days. "Hey," he continued. "Was that you whistling out there last night?"

The guard laughed. "No way. Wasn't anybody whistling around here. There was a lot of screaming and swearing across the hall, but these cells are pretty soundproof, so you may not have heard it. That's why we call it solitary."

"Oh," Bruce said, as the slot slammed shut. "Thanks."

He sat down and began to pick at his breakfast. "And we used to think hospital food was bad," he joked to himself. Then he paused. Who could have been whistling? By now the song was firmly embedded in his mind, and he began to hum it to himself as he turned over the possibilities in his mind. Suddenly he realized why the tune was so familiar. It was from one of those tapes his wife had played over and over again. He quit humming and sang the words to the last few lines: "I will be with you, I will be with you, because that's who I AM."

Suddenly a smile broke across his face. Of course! It wasn't the guard; it wasn't any prisoners. These were soundproof walls.

"Thank You," Bruce whispered. "Thank You that I'm not alone in here, and thank You for keeping Your promise about singing me songs in the night. And thank You for this breakfast. After all, You promised only my bread and water would be sure, and they do have that." Bruce chuckled to himself, and for the first time in weeks he actually felt happy.

As I recorded the events in the lives of Mike's family, it struck me how powerful their prayers were. With every prayer and with every request for help, more guardians swarmed to their side, and the more difficult the demonic task of breaking down their trust became.

Silently, with no earthly fanfare, our Prince stood up in the Most Holy Place, and in an instant the three family members were sealed. Their battle was over. They belonged to Him. Now, all that was left was the victory celebration. They just didn't know it yet. They were still prisoners on earth, but it was almost over. I could barely contain my excitement.

EPILOGUE

Suddenly the entire earth convulsed as if in a grand seizure. The sea seemed to roar and boil and crash up onto the land. Inhabited islands sank and disappeared. Mountains seemed to melt down into the earth, while valleys were thrown up like volcanic eruptions. The dead were thrown out of their sleeping places, and many began to rise through the air.

The clouds crashed together in the sky and suddenly opened to reveal our Prince with thousands of angels. Bruce was thrown from his cot in the cell. The penitentiary crumbled about him as he began to rise through the air. Farther up, he caught sight of his wife, looking radiant, healthy, and glowing as she rose through the air.

Mike was awakened with the earthquake. Pete grabbed his hand. "Come on, Mike," he said, "it's time to go."

"Pete?" Mike asked. Suddenly Pete looked much taller and broader and radiant. In fact, his robe was so bright that it hurt Mike's eyes. "Pete?" he asked again.

"Yes," said Pete. "I've been your guardian. I am your guardian. You didn't have to go through this alone, you know." Mike hung on tightly as he and Pete rose through the air.

Don woke from a sound sleep. The tall Arab who had befriended him was shaking him by the shoulder. "Wake up, Don," he said. "It's over. It's time to go home."

"You speak English?" Don asked incredulously.

"Of course," he laughed. "I've been with you since before you were born! Come on, Jesus is waiting for us!"

"Jesus?" Don said.

With another crash the mountain split open. Don didn't even have to crawl out through the tiny opening of the cave; he and several others who had hidden with him rose through the air to meet their Lord.

The little family that had been separated by death and by distance now clasped hands. They began to babble all at once and then stopped. Who could talk about other things right now? They all turned their eyes on Jesus. He was the only way they had survived.

The war was over! And my job was over. All I had to do now was record the happy ending.

Mark

THE WATCHERS' BANQUET

I stood at the door welcoming the humans to the banquet hall. All of them were accompanied by their personal guardians. When all had been seated, I began:

"Welcome to the watchers' banquet. By now you have all gotten a chance to be with Jesus and have been able to meet your friends and families you were separated from. If you haven't had enough time with the King yet, don't be distressed. None of us ever have. We all find that the more time we spend with Him, the more we want. You have all of eternity to do this.

"I was your immortal watcher. I kept the records of your lives and the choices you made during your time on earth. All over heaven the other watchers and I are hosting these banquets to answer your questions and help you understand what really happened. We will make all of the archives available to you and will answer any questions you have.

"Your guardians are not the only angels invited to our banquet. As you know, we are spirits and take this form so you can see us comfortably. While your guardians may not look familiar to you right now, just watch."

Monique turned to her guardian. Something strange was happening. He was changing from the tall shining being to a short arthritic old man. She squealed in delight! "Uncle Francois! You were an angel?" She flung her arms around him. "Oh, thank you! Thank you!

"And look!" she cried. "You were the soldiers who brought us food that Christmas Day when we had nothing left to eat! How could we have been afraid of you?"

Marcus watched as two of the beings were transformed into his cellmates from the Mamertine prison in Rome. "You were with me the whole time!" he whispered in amazement.

"Of course," his guardian replied. "Our Prince promised you that you would never be alone, and you never were."

Each of the guests exclaimed in surprise as the guardians were changed into forms of people they recognized—people who had encouraged, taught, helped, fed, and rescued them.

As the humans watched the archives of their lives they were surprised and delighted at finally seeing behind the scenes. "I had no idea there were bandits waiting for us in those hills across the river," Miriam said. "You guardians took care of them, and we never even saw them!"

"And what about that big chunk of ceiling and those bullets?" Don commented. "You had your wings over me, and I was as safe as a bug in a rug and didn't even see them aiming for me and bouncing off!"

"We have another surprise for you," I continued. "Often the Almighty used you to save others. Usually humans don't know the results of their efforts, and sometimes they don't even know the good they have done. We want to show you some of these results here."

The translucent walls turned into giant projection screens as the faces appeared: those Geoffrey saved by smuggling them out of France, those whom Joe helped escape from the Roman soldiers, and countless more.

"When you were welcomed here, our Prince gave each of you a crown. You will notice that each one is different. Each one has a special personal meaning that represents your relationship with Jesus. The stone in the front carries the special new name He has given you. There is a matching stone on the High Priest's breast-plate that He wears over His heart. Your stone is new to you, but He has carried you over His heart all this time." The humans audibly caught their breath as they marveled at His long-term love He had literally carried for them.

"You will also notice that your crowns have many other stones and jewels in them. They are miniatures of the personal stones He has given to others. Each of the stones in your crown represents a person you helped bring to Jesus." Some humans had only their own personal stone in their crowns. Other crowns—like Peter's, Megan's, and Rachel's—seemed to be completely gem-crusted.

"Our best surprise, though, is to give you special personal time with the One who made all of this possible. It is with great pleasure that I present the King of kings, Lord of lords, King of creation, and the greatest Lover in the universe: Jesus!"

The cheer was overwhelming. "Jesus! Jesus! Jesus!" cried the redeemed as they rushed forward. Pulling their crowns off, they threw them at His feet. "We don't deserve these! You deserve them all! You are just awesome!"

And we angels have to agree. But, then, we have always known that God is love! We back off shyly, because even though we have known Him for millennia, the intense intimate relationship He has with these humans He died to save—well, it leaves us breathless. We drift together humming that little human ditty: "God is love; God is love. Praise Him, praise Him, all ye little children, God is love, God is love."